ANIMAL HUSBANDRY

AND OTHER FICTIONS

JEFF FLEISCHER

RUNNING WILD

Animal Husbandry
text copyright © remains with author
Edited by Benjamin White
All rights reserved.

Published in North America and Europe by Running Wild Press. Visit Running
Wild Press at www.runningwildpress.com Educators, librarians, book clubs (as
well as the eternally curious), go to
www.runningwildpress.com.
ISBN (pbk) 978-1-960018-06-9
ISBN (ebook) 978-1-960018-05-2

CONTENTS

ANIMAL HUSBANDRY

At around two in the afternoon, on an otherwise unimportant Tuesday in June, Herm Dublin's prize heifer gave birth.

It happened the way such things normally did. She'd been heavy with a calf for some time, and Dublin looked forward to the birth the way all small, organic dairy farmers did. A pregnant heifer was a heifer who'd soon be producing a lot of milk, and a calf meant a potential future source of even more milk. Dublin's farm was hardly in trouble, but a successful birth was always welcome. When the time came, the heifer began to grunt loudly, and several minutes later she'd expelled her offspring onto the ground behind her, a trail of vibrant red afterbirth still hanging off her flanks.

One motorist driving by honked in a salute of congratulations, and a semi passing the other way did likewise. Herm Dublin smiled and tipped his broad-brimmed hat. Word usually traveled fast between the farms in that part of the countryside, and it wouldn't be long before some of his neighbors would stop by to see the new addition to his herd. Herm looked over toward his heifer's scion, who was still covered in the mother's blood and taking a while to get upright. Dublin couldn't get a clear view from where he was weeding on the other side of the paddock, but the amount of effort the heifer put into cleaning and nudging her offspring worried him that the calf might be stillborn. Still, Dublin knew his way around cattle, and knew to give her some space until the baby was standing.

Dublin's friend Jim O'Hara, who owned the soybean farm down the road, came strolling by, whistling a familiar sea shanty. He was dressed for the field, in his overalls and mesh cap, and had long ago mastered the ability to whistle clearly even while chewing a large plug of wintergreen tobacco. "Looks like you got a plenty big calf there," he called out to Dublin.

"Yep. Fresh one, too," Dublin said, ambling over as the younger man hopped the painted-wood fence. The two clasped hands, and O'Hara offered Dublin a chaw, which he declined as always with a wave of his hand.

When Dublin looked back at the calf, however, something seemed off. The former heifer had given up her quest to make it stand, and instead grazed near some of the other cows. The young animal wasn't stillborn as Dublin had initially feared, as it moved against the ground on its own, but its mother hadn't bothered to finish cleaning it. A cow giving up on a living calf was something neither man had ever seen before, and they knew there had to be a reason. They discovered it quickly.

The calf had fully formed horns on its head. They were still in proportion to the animal's size, but it usually took the better part of a year for a Holstein bull to grow horns like that. Then, there was the body. Which wasn't calf-like at all, but almost human. Covered in bristly black and white fur, sure, and with hooves. The torso, though, was definitely human-ish in the tightness of its ribs and the curve of its spine, and the front shoulders were set so that the front legs could hang on the calf's sides. Even the animal's head was wrong somehow. He — and both farmers could see it was a he — had the big black eyes of a cow, only they faced forward with the binocular gaze of a hunter, rather than sit in sockets on the side of the head, the way the eyes of a prey animal should.

O'Hara let out a long whistle, and nearly swallowed his plug of tobacco. "I'll be darned. Looks like you got yourself some kind of cow-boy. Only time I ever seen one of them was back in Davenport when I was a kid." He was thinking of a traveling sideshow that his parents had taken him to see on one of their summer driving trips through the Midwest. "Thing weren't much bigger than this one. It was all like preserved, in a big jar. Didn't look this real, though... Hadn't thought about that in years."

Dublin wasn't nearly as calm about the situation, but tried to match his friend's ease on the surface. "This ain't natural," he said, shaking his head. His mind had already made the inevitable, awful jump. If this cow really was part boy, or if it was a boy that was part cow, then that meant his prize heifer had the kind of encounter he didn't even want to picture. All he knew for sure was it wasn't his own doing.

The calf, or whatever it was, still squirmed in the way of a newborn child, and started to cry. It wasn't the wail of a normal human baby, but it also wasn't the sound of a regular calf. Instead, it was something otherworldly, guttural, and pained.

O'Hara was a grain farmer by trade, but grew up in a dairy family and still maintained a keen interest in animal husbandry. "Better get the cow-boy out of there," he suggested. "It keeps on bawling like that, it's gonna spook the others. Can't have your milk getting sour."

Herm thought the point well taken, and grabbed an armful

of towels from one of the clotheslines he kept near the fence. He began to dry the blood from the writhing animal while his friend continued to pontificate, "I remember my old man telling me about the time that coyote came around. Said the howling scared the whole herd, they was on edge for days, twitchy. Maybe a whole month's worth of milk must've gone bad..."

Herm Dublin had dried the calf — he still wanted to think of it as a deformed calf, rather than the monstrous hybrid it so obviously was — and swaddled it as gently as he could with the remaining clean towels. He held the animal a short distance away from his body, which proved wise as one of the horns grazed his right shoulder and left a stinging but unserious scrape. He carried it over to the fence where O'Hara stood. His friend examined the animal closely, at once fascinated and repulsed by its oddity, but the animal cried when he tried to touch it. Jim spat out some tobacco juice and tried not to stare at the hybrid's cold, black eyes. It continued to cry, and both men felt shivers as they heard that unnatural sound up close.

Not knowing what else to do with it, they decided to show the animal to Old Zed, the country veterinarian, who lived only about half a mile down the road. Zed had never much cared for the telephone — "If it's important enough to bother me, it's important enough to come find me," he always said — and the two farmers figured he'd deem this important enough to bother him. Besides, finding him was never that hard. Zed rarely left his plot, unless it was to make a house call in the area. He was never gone long, and usually came home straight away.

Sure enough, they found Zed in the handmade rocking chair on his porch, reading an old detective novel while his bloodhound, Jolene, slept at his feet. "Hey boys," he greeted them. Zed's bones creaked nearly as much as his old chair, and O'Hara and Dublin were next to him before he had time to get up. He tipped his fishing hat to them and leaned back, starting the chair to rock again. Before he could say anything else, the bundle in Dublin's arms made a plaintive noise, and Zed's hound dog jumped up. The old girl turned, pushed the swinging screen door to the house open, and darted inside as the door slammed behind her from the motion. Zed laughed a bit, and looked with interest at the cow-headed boy his friend carried.

"Well, I'll be," he said with a broad smile. "Looks like you boys got yourselves a minotaur. I never seen one of these in the flesh before. How'd you come across it?"

Herm Dublin told the old man how he came to own this unusual beast, and how he wasn't sure what exactly to do with it, and how he didn't want to chance spoiling his year's yield by spooking all his cows.

"Nah, that's just one of them urban legends," Zed said, as O'Hara looked surprised. "I reckon they'll be fine, just maybe a bit confused."

As he spoke, the old vet instinctively began to examine the hybrid infant. He held his index finger against its dewlap to check the heartbeat, then moved the finger slowly in front of the eyes to make sure the animal tracked its movement properly. The only time the vet registered surprise was when he opened the animal's mouth, and found a cow's thick tongue in a mouth full of primate teeth. "Now that's right strange," he said. "These teeth are too sharp for grazing, and with the body the way it is, I'll reckon the stomach's not got all the right parts anyway."

"Nothing about it's right," Herm Dublin said, smiling at his friends while still regarding the animal in his arms with a sense of horror, a sense that this minotaur was wholly unnatural. Herm Dublin wasn't the most pious man around — he hadn't gone to church in years — but he figured nothing good could come from anything this human-ish with horns. His younger friend, however, continued to regard it with curiosity, like this cow-boy living and breathing among them was no different than the deformed bull fetus in a jar of formaldehyde at the sideshow. "Why's he keep yelling like that?" O'Hara asked when the vet removed his hands from the animal's mouth and received another wail in response.

Old Zed pondered the question for a minute, then laughed. "That's an easy one. Poor thing's a couple hours old already, and ain't had anything to eat." He went into the house for a few minutes and returned with a glass bottle of raw milk.

The minotaur cried hysterically when he saw it. He tried to reach for it the way a human baby would reach for a bottle, but his hooves stopped him from gripping and holding it. The vet took the swaddled animal in his arms and poured the milk into the oddly formed mouth, where the minotaur's thick tongue lapped it up.

The screen door swung open, and Zed's daughter Angie joined them. She was only in town for the summer before heading back to school come September. Angie had always been a bright girl, the first of Zed's long line of offspring to go off to college, and still had a whole mess of books up in her room. "What you got there, Daddy?" she asked. "I didn't know anybody around here was expecting..." She stopped mid-sentence when she saw the horned child.

"I was just expecting a calf," Herm Dublin said somewhat apologetically, wondering if this animal would feed the same way a normal calf did, and again thinking how wrong that would look. "Just a plain old ordinary calf. Instead, my cow gives birth to this here minotaur. Not quite sure what to do with it; figured your pa might have some ideas."

"I might; I read about one of these in one of my classes," the girl said, noticing that Old Zed beamed with pride at hearing his daughter sound so smart. "I'm not sure it's a minotaur. I think that's if a woman, like a person woman, has a baby with a bull. Sounds like a man had a baby with your cow."

Everyone laughed at that, except Herm Dublin, who didn't like being reminded of it.

"Tell you what," she offered. "I think I got a book about 'em. Hold on."

The girl went back inside for just a few minutes, while the cow-boy finished his milk and the three men continued to regard the animal's odd face. The minotaur had stopped crying, but there was still something in its eyes that made Dublin uncomfortable. A sense that, even when its appetite was satisfied, it had a feral, inhuman quality. Herm Dublin had lived around animals his whole life, and he knew that all of them — especially dogs and cats and pigs, but even cows — had a softness in their eyes, a look that told you something about their individual personalities.

This animal didn't have that.

Angie came back with a book, and handed it to Dublin. It was a ragged, used textbook she had left over from a high school literature class, with a bunch of pen markings all over it, and a few visibly torn pages. "There's a story in here all about a minotaur that used to live in Greece," she said. "Figure it can be like an instruction book for you, all about how to raise one. Been a while since I read it, but might have some good pointers."

Dublin thanked the girl, while O'Hara took the cow-boy from Old Zed, and the two of them walked back to the Dublin farm. The rest of the cows — or rightly, Dublin figured, all the cows, since this wasn't really one — were still grazing, but it was getting late in the day and he had to start milking. He and O'Hara made a pile of straw in the barn for the minotaur, a place where Herm could keep an eye on it while milking the others, but where it would otherwise stay out of sight of the other animals. While Herm busied himself with his work, Jim took the textbook home to read up on how to take care of a minotaur, promising he'd return the next day with some ideas.

By the time O'Hara showed in the morning, the minotaur calf had started to find its wobbly legs. It could only get up on them for a few seconds before falling down, making it still a lot slower than a normal calf, but still far ahead of the pace for a normal human baby. It was comfortable enough that it could sometimes stay upright for a few minutes and lick up raw milk from a short-rimmed bucket Dublin had left for it, but it spent most of its time moving about awkwardly in the pile of straw the farmer had put together.

"How'd your reading go?" Herm Dublin asked his friend, as they cooked eggs and potatoes in skillets on his back porch. "Think we can get a handle on what to do with this here minotaur?"

Jim O'Hara took a deep breath. Sure as his word, he'd gone home and read everything about the minotaur in the book, and now he was starting to share his friend's suspicion that this thing wasn't just unusual, but flat out wasn't right. "Now, I don't rightly know how much of this book is true," he began, spitting before he continued. "I never read nothing else about them, but some of this just shouldn't be."

Dublin nodded, urging his friend to keep on, but O'Hara seemed nervous about continuing.

"Thing is, according to this book, a minotaur...well, a minotaur eats people."

"That don't make sense. It's got a cow's head, and a cow don't eat people, or even eat meat," Dublin said. He knew some of the bigger, non-organic farms did feed their cows a bunch of cheap feed that had ground-up cow parts in it, but he knew that wasn't right either. "And the other half's a person, and people don't eat people."

"Book says it does it cause a minotaur's unnatural, and it has to do unnatural stuff. Lots of unnatural stuff. Says the minotaur's supposed to live in a big maze that he can't figure a way out of, and you're supposed to feed him seven men and seven women." He continued, with a severe look on his face. "They gotta all be virgins and they gotta go into his maze alive so he can kill 'em himself. Book says every nine years, but then there's another part saying it might be every year. Doesn't seem rightly sure."

"I reckon it's gotta be every year. It can't go nine years without eating..." Herm Dublin trailed off, and O'Hara wasn't sure what to say either.

The two farmers ate their eggs and potatoes in silence, but both were thinking the same thing. They couldn't in good conscience feed people to the minotaur. Maybe there were some criminals who might deserve a fate like that, but neither of them knew of any criminals who were virgins. Around their part of the countryside, folks still had children pretty young, and just about everyone left school with at least some experience. The ones who didn't tended not to be the criminal type.

Herm Dublin did have one idea. "Maybe it's best if we kill it," he said with an air of resignation. "Can't rightly let fourteen people die every year just to keep one person alive. Especially if it's only kind of a person." Even as he said it, he wondered if it would be murder — if the act would count as slaughtering a bull or killing an unarmed boy.

O'Hara's face fell. He'd been troubled by what he'd read in the book, but he also found it interesting. He knew he didn't want to let anybody die to feed the minotaur, but he also didn't want to kill him. Like that one in the jar, this animal was different, was special. While his friend couldn't escape the idea of some strange man creating this outcome, O'Hara wondered if the minotaur hadn't come from something else, like some next

9

step in evolution or some new part of creation. Didn't seem right to get rid of it, at least not yet, especially if it was the only one. "For now, he's only drinking milk," he began, noting that he called the minotaur *him* when he talked, while Dublin always used *it*. "Reckon it'll be a while before he needs, well, solid food. No reason not to see what happens natural."

Dublin nodded, and Jim O'Hara knew he'd bought the animal some time. For the next few weeks, the minotaur continued to live in the farmer's barn, drinking raw milk, growing larger, getting more comfortable on its legs. All four at first, but by Indian summer the minotaur had started to walk on two legs, hunched but mostly upright. Old Zed would drop by from time to time to check on the minotaur's health, and Angie would hand feed it apples or carrots, stroking the animal's broad, cold nose. There was too much cow in the minotaur for it to speak properly, but both Dublin and O'Hara grew to know the meanings of its grunts and moans.

Herm Dublin realized after some time that he'd somehow grown attached to the beast that once horrified him. He still saw no look of recognition in the minotaur's black eyes, but he often found himself patting its coarse fur and starting to think of the animal, if not as a friend or even a pet, as something different and special. Like O'Hara, he started to think of the minotaur as *him*, and the idea of killing him gradually moved to the back of the farmer's mind. By the end of September, however, the minotaur had grown to the size of a healthy human teenager, and it became clear even to Jim O'Hara that the question of the animal's future would have to be decided soon. The time for that decision came without warning on a cool Monday evening, when a boy from the local high school came by to haul away some scrap metal for a few dollars.

Dublin wasn't entirely sure what happened, but the boy must've cut himself pretty bad on one of the rusty sheets of corrugated scrap as he threw it on the back of his truck. Almost as soon as the blood started running down the boy's arm, Dublin could hear the guttural cry of his special hybrid from the barn, as if he smelled and wanted what must have been virginal blood. Within seconds, the minotaur broke out of the barn and ran at the young man, who stood too frozen in shock to react as the creature charged toward him with the speed of an enraged bull and the bloodlust of a feral man.

The farmer could only watch from the window as his strange charge ripped the boy apart, with both horns and hooves, and began to consume him in a frenzy. Dublin knew there was nothing he could do, as his fear of interrupting the chaos overwhelmed his curiosity and kept him an observer at the window. The animal ate quickly and without a break, as if it had gone days without food. Once done, the minotaur got up and walked to the barn with the calm gait of an accomplished and satiated man, leaving behind a grotesque pile of bone and meat.

Still not quite believing what he'd seen, Dublin eased out his back door and ran down the road in the direction of O'Hara's soybean farm. He was careful to stay in the shadows, making sure he was never in the sightline of his own barn, and trying to avoid the attentions of any passing drivers who might have seen something. O'Hara's farm was barely a mile away, but the run seemed to Dublin to take forever, between the physical stress of the run on his ample frame and the mental stress of having no real plan of action.

He found his friend reading the newspaper in his hammock, and O'Hara nearly jumped from the sling when he saw Dublin drenched in sweat and shaking from terror. After catching his breath, the dairy farmer recounted the horror of what he'd just seen, realizing its reality as he described it aloud. Neither man could deny that this turn of events wasn't right, and that it was time to do something drastic. They drove O'Hara's pickup down to Old Zed's place, sure he would know what had to be done, and easily found the creaky veterinarian asleep in his rocking chair.

When the three men arrived at the Dublin farm, they could hear that the minotaur was asleep in the barn, breathing heavily from the weight of its overfilled belly. The cattle had clearly been spooked by the whole ordeal, as nearly all of them had taken their sleeping stances along the far end of the paddock, as close to the fence opposite the barn as their instincts could get them. The poor prize heifer seemed particularly troubled, still awake and absently turning herself in circles against the fenced perimeter, seeming not to notice she was repeatedly scraping her side on a loose board.

Zed was the first to enter the barn. His movements woke the minotaur, but the animal didn't show any aggression, or move much at all. It just looked at the vet with the same neutral expression the men had all come to know. "There, there," the vet said as he took a long needle from his gunny sack and proceeded to give the tired animal a shot of tranquilizer. It was a large dose, enough to put most animals under, but the minotaur's body was unusually thick and strong.

"Reckon this will do the trick, but he might still be awake," Old Zed said. "Now's as good a time as any to end this." Unable to watch the inevitable, the vet placed a hand on the dairy farmer's shoulder and headed out to the road. He hummed to himself as he walked home, unconsciously trying to drown out the sound that would come any second, as he thought about what he'd say about that evening the next time his daughter called him from school.

Once the old man had departed, Herm Dublin took down the rifle he kept on hooks inside the barn wall, the one he usually used just to scare the coyotes away. He loaded the gun in the usual manner, pumped it once, and prepared to farewell the calf he'd so anticipated not that long ago. Dublin looked into the animal's black eyes, which showed no sign of the comprehension he'd see in a dog or cat or pig, or even a cow. He raised the gun, but he just couldn't do it. This just wasn't right.

He and O'Hara knew they had to take some action soon, as the tranquilizer would only last so long, and neither knew what would happen once the powerful animal came to or if it would comprehend what they were doing. After whispering to each other for a few minutes, the two farmers settled on a plan. It was one O'Hara had mentioned in passing several days earlier, after he'd reread the key sections of Angie's textbook. He wasn't rightly serious when he'd suggested it, but he did note it was a solution that would prevent them from having to make a terrible choice. The way he'd put it was that maybe the minotaur was supposed to live, and maybe that meant it had to feed, but that didn't mean *they* had to be the ones to feed it.

Jim O'Hara had thought about the maze in the book, the one where the minotaur lived but couldn't find a way out, and how there was a maze like that not all that far from them. The Davidson farm the next town over was the kind of farm that didn't actually grow anything anymore, but got passed down through a family that liked living in a big farmhouse and having the land to themselves. The old owners had planted their hedge rows in a tricky pattern, and over generations the maze had become a tourist draw for the whole county. The Davidsons added more layers every few years, until the thing took up quite a few hectares. Just about anyone who ever wandered in had to call one of the Davidsons to help them find their way out, and the whole thing was fenced in so that the family could charge admission during the summer.

Dublin figured that was where the cow-boy belonged, in as close to his natural state as such an unnatural animal could exist. He and O'Hara carefully dragged the sedated minotaur from the barn, past the spooked cows in the paddock. With great effort they lifted the animal into the back of Dublin's truck and strapped it down, just in case the tranquilizer wore off too soon. They drove in silence through the dusk, across the quiet county line, eventually coming to the Davidson farm's maze. Knowing that they couldn't exactly ask permission for what they were doing, they carefully lifted the animal from the truck, dropped it onto a wheeled flatbed O'Hara kept in the backseat, and took a spool of fishline to help them find their own way out of the maze.

Together, the two farmers maneuvered the sedated minotaur through the brackets and twists of the thick, metal-framed hedge rows, trailing the fishline behind them. They made sure to double back, to take wrong turns, whatever they could to further disorient the pitiful but powerful cow-boy on the off chance it was paying attention. When the spool showed they had run out of line, the farmers slid the minotaur off the flatbed and onto the soft soil in the midst of the hedges. O'Hara was too sad to do more than tip his cap to the unique animal, but Dublin bent down, rubbed the calf's nose, and took one more look into the eyes he now thought of as unmarked rather than blank. While the minotaur was still too drugged to move, the two men followed their line back to the end of the maze, winding it back on the spool as they went. They packed up their supplies and prepared to leave, but Dublin realized they had one more task at hand. He ripped a page out of the road atlas in the pickup's glove compartment and scribbled a thorough note to leave on the Davidsons' door, anonymously warning them about their horticultural creation's new purpose and the true nature of its new resident, and urging them not to enter the maze anymore. After all, it wouldn't have been right not to warn them. Neither Herm Dublin nor Jim O'Hara ever went back to the maze, and the two men vowed never to tell anyone else about the minotaur or what they did with it.

Dublin never found out how or why his heifer came to give birth to that calf, or how long the hybrid animal survived on its own. There were rumors, from time to time, that a high school boy who reckoned he had something to prove had disappeared in the maze, or that farmers sleeping out on a hot night had heard the guttural cry of the minotaur, or even that the warning note — and the story it told — was just something the David-sons had cooked up to stop teenage couples from using their property for extracurricular activity. Those rumors lasted a long time, a whole lot longer than most cows ever lasted. Dublin never knew if it was the minotaur itself, or just the fear and curiosity its cries had inspired, that was keeping the rumors alive.

Each time one of his heifers grew heavy with a calf, Herm Dublin feared another minotaur was about to enter his world, even as part of him shared Jim O'Hara's hope of getting another glimpse at another oddity. Each time a calf was born, both men had to admit, even if only to each other, that they were a little disappointed by the animal's normal form. Both knew that feeling just wasn't right, but it also felt sort of natural.

THE QUERULOUS NIGHTINGALE

I arrived in Washington the same day that James Forrestal went out the window.

My first visit to the capital would have been otherwise forgettable. Union Station was less crowded on a Sunday morning than I'd ever found a stateside train station. Never a churchgoing man myself, I still felt a nostalgia for the chiming bells I periodically passed on the way from the train to the Mayflower Hotel.

They told me I'd been abroad too long.

* * *

"Welcome to the Mayflower. How may I help you?" the old man behind the desk greeted me.

"Douglas, room for one." As he searched the reservation list with his finger, I took a moment to examine the lobby's chandelier and the reliefs that surrounded it, the carved figures emerging a few inches from the wall.

"Here it is. Douglas. Room's paid for two weeks; if you plan to stay longer, let us know beforehand. We have a few months until the busy season, so you should be fine."

I nodded as he rang the bell and produced a bellhop not much younger than me. I could tell from the way his left arm hung limp that he'd seen combat; only a field medic would have both been able to save the arm and lacked enough time to set it properly.

"Take your bags, sir?"

I held up the sole bag I carried. "I'll bring this up myself."

"Then right this way, sir." The bellhop had a slight hitch in his step, which combined with the arm to remind me of a production of *Richard III* I'd seen before the war. "Mind if I smoke?" he asked.

"I'll join you." I intended to light his cigarette before my own, but he produced a match and struck it with his good hand before I could remove my matchbook from my suit pocket. He managed the elevator with similar dexterity but must have noticed my glancing at his arm.

"Best years of our lives, right?" He smiled and took another puff. "Got this from one of Hirohito's snipers on Tarawa in '43. They had to load us on a raft and float us out to a ship for treatment. Took long enough that the bullet moved around and there was nerve damage."

"You get the guy who did it?"

"Him and two of his sidekicks."

"Paid back with interest. Well done."

"You look like you served."

I nodded, but took a long drag on my Lucky rather than divulge any more information. When we got to my floor, I told the bellhop I would take myself the rest of the way. He handed me a copper key, and I passed him a dollar, making eye contact and shaking his hand firmly as I did so.

17

* * *

The room provided more space than I would ever need, with a bed thrice the size of any of the spartan arrangements to which I'd grown accustomed, and a fabric armchair like the one my father sat in whenever he would listen to his serials.

I threw my suit coat and hat on the oak writing desk and took off my shoes, which had given me a small but painful blister on my right heel. On the nightstand sat a bottle of Kentucky bourbon, serving as a paperweight for the brown-paper envelope with *Welcome Home* scrawled on it by an anonymous woman's pen. There wasn't much chance of finding a bar open on Sunday.

Out of habit, I checked the bourbon to make sure the wax seal was unbroken before pouring myself a glass. The oaky flavor met my tongue like a reunited friend, but the stuffy room had left the bottle too warm. In my stocking feet, I took a walk down the hall to buy a cold soda as a mixer.

Though the rooms on both sides of mine seemed empty, as promised, I heard low voices coming from the next room down. Just two French-Canadian women discussing lunch plans; nothing to worry about. I found the soda, then returned to my chambers to pour myself a drink.

From the window, I had my first view of the White House. It looked smaller than it had always seemed in *The March of Time*, but what struck me was its condition. Time away had made my homeland feel prefabricated, as if I were looking at a sanitized replica of the very ruins in Thessaly or Epirus that I'd played a small role in keeping part of the free world.

At that moment, Truman was probably taking some important meeting inside those sandstone walls, Louis Johnson was still settling into his new job, and, I would soon learn, his predecessor's broken body was being examined somewhere in Bethesda.

* * *

Monday arrived later for me than it should have, my internal clock having yet to reset and my memories of the night before a haze of bourbon and the contents of the package left for me.

The hotel shower with its cleansing force felt like a luxury, and even the commode provided comfort I hadn't experienced in some time, though this had more to do with the quiet and solitude than the facilities. When I finished toweling myself, I found a sheet of paper had been slipped under the door, telling me the time and place of my evening appointment. I checked the hallway, but whoever delivered it had already gone.

The city was busier, with men in suits on their way to work, a pattern into which my small bag and I blended easily. The note had given me several hours to kill, and I thought the guise of a tourist was that least likely to prompt notice of an unattached man free on a workday.

I carried my camera around my neck, and made a show of taking a panorama of images — the Washington Monument, the Lincoln Memorial, the Capitol dome in the distance — all the while surveying the evening's meeting place and taking mental notes. I knew the value of understanding one's surroundings.

Having already thrown the last of my drachma in a trash can far from the hotel, and sure nobody was close enough to see, I took the old identification cards I carried and wrapped them around my next Lucky. As the match head burned them away, their ashes spread over the reflecting pool like tiny birds on the wing.

* * *

I took supper in a small diner near the Old Ebbitt, choosing the stool farthest from the door, at the end of a long and nearly empty counter. After ordering, I purchased an *Evening Star* from the rack up front, and opened to the Clifford Berryman cartoon while sampling the too-thick coffee.

Flipping through the afternoon paper was how I first heard the news about the old warhorse's plunge out the window of a hospital few knew had become his home. Of course, I'd heard rumors about his mental state and his paranoia, as everyone in our line of work had, but never knew how much of that to believe.

"Put 'em in a box, tie 'em with a ribbon, and throw 'em in the deep blue sea," the waitress said as she refilled my coffee.

"I'm sorry?"

"That's the song," she said, indicating the Wurlitzer in the corner. "You looked like you were trying to figure out what it was. It's Doris Day."

"Thank you. I'm afraid I don't know much about music." I returned to my paper, looking for more clues about the Forrestal story as I dipped my toast in the mix of runny eggs and burnt potatoes the waitress had brought over. I could feel her eyes on me while I read, but kept my head down to avoid any unneeded conversation.

While paying my bill, I considered the turning dessert display next to the register, and opted for two pieces of fresh Turkish delight and a small block of halva to take back to my hotel.

"Who's that man in the paper you keep looking at?" the waitress asked as she counted my change. "Somebody important?"

"Paper says his name was James Forrestal," I said, feigning

ignorance. "He was the first secretary of defense. He just killed himself."

"Sounds like you don't know much about government either." It could have sounded mean, but she smiled when she said it, showing off. "Henry Knox had that job for George Washington."

"Knox was the first secretary of war," I said. "This man was the first secretary of defense."

"Sounds like the same job to me. What's the difference?"

"The difference is all the difference."

* * *

With several hours remaining before my scheduled rendezvous, I returned to the Mayflower to shower and rest. I nodded a greeting to the bellhop, but bypassed the elevator to take the stairs. I again checked the doors surrounding mine for noise and, finding none, let myself in.

Closing the door, I did not expect to see my room already occupied.

The man sitting in the desk chair wore sunglasses, and his left leg jutted out at an unnatural angle. Though I pulled my gun from my suit's inner pocket, his was already aimed directly at the doorway where I stood. The older man perched on the bed rose when I entered, and smiled.

"Urge him with truth to frame his fair replies," he said, lighting a cigarette.

"And sure he will, for wisdom never lies," I responded. The man with the weapon put his away, and I followed suit. "What are you doing here?"

"We moved your debrief to a more secure location."

After I first saw the gun, I thought of the whispers about former operatives being eliminated, and kept my guard. "Can I smoke?" I asked, waiting for a nod before taking out my Luckys and lighting one.

"Now, we've reviewed your file, and are familiar with your work for the agency," the older man said. "As you know, we're not technically supposed to operate on American soil, so everything we say here stays between us."

"Understood. I—"

"We want to get to know you a bit before handing out any new assignments," the other interrupted. "To do that, we want to get more familiar with what led you to the agency, why you wanted the job, why you're a fit. Most men with your background went the career-military route after the war, but not you." He named the most recent assignments in my file, as if I were unfamiliar with them, feigning admiration while I smoked and nodded to show I was paying attention.

Eventually, they gave me a chance to explain how I'd watched the same war films most men my age had, and eagerly joined the war only to find the reality of combat a less glorious enterprise. I detailed how, both philosophically and tactically, I preferred eliminating individual targets who had earned it rather than dozens of ordinary men whose only mistake was being born on the wrong soil.

I liked to think of myself as a precision instrument, and my experience confirmed that impression.

The older man kept his questions informational, while the one with the wonky leg peppered me with confrontational queries: "How did you feel about keeping the world safe for democracy by putting a king in charge?" "What would you have done if Wallace won last fall?" "How do we know so much time talking to the DSE didn't turn you a little pink?"

I answered every question, with cold but professional precision. Smokers were always easier to read; whatever disguises their faces formed when speaking had a tendency to relent slightly while they focused on their habit. I insisted on asking a few of my own questions, about the possible next stations, how our work had been perceived on the homefront, if these men had heard anything about any of my men who had already come home. Both insisted they either didn't know or couldn't tell me any of those things.

Then I settled on a question I'd been thinking about for most of the day.

"Last words have always fascinated me," I said. "Since you know the password, you must be in position to know. What were Forrestal's last words?" Neither answered. "Surely, if it were a suicide, he left a note; and surely you must know what it said. Unless you're not who you say you are."

The older man fielded this one. "He was copying a translation of a Sophocles play, and left off at 'No quiet murmur like the tremulous wail, of the lone bird, the querulous nightingale.' One of the experts from Annapolis said it's about suicide."

"I know the play. It's about the suicide of Ajax, after he goes mad, butchering and torturing sheep and cattle."

"That makes sense," the older man said. "Forrestal went mad almost as soon as he was fired. It was only a matter of time."

I thought about what he said for a few minutes, then asked permission to pour myself a drink from the bourbon bottle. I offered a beverage to each of my interviewers, who agreed only after they saw me swallow my own serving.

The following afternoon, I sat with my sole bag outside Union Station, waiting for the California-bound train I planned to inconspicuously exit at one of its refueling stops.

Smoking the last of my cigarettes, I thought about why last

words had always mattered to me. I'd grown to dislike the kind of war movies I grew up watching. They had no realism, and offered only two ways to die. Men were shot and fell to the ground like pieces of wood, dead but clean, or they received a slow death that let them deliver their final thoughts, urgently and masterfully, then fall silent the instant they finished imparting their wisdom.

In my war experience, nobody knew when their last moment was coming. Usually, soldiers' last words were screams of pain or vain calls for their mothers.

Despite the interviewers' assumptions, my post-war activities for the agency hadn't turned me pink. Only angry.

I was grateful to my contact for the file detailing how the other members of my team had been murdered within a few days of their own Washington debriefs, and warning me about my visitors — had they pantomimed grief for my compatriots instead of ignorance, I might not have deciphered their intentions. Though I had never admired Forrestal, who always seemed extreme and obsessed, I saw no reason for what happened to him and wanted to gauge what my would-be executioners thought. Whether he was killed directly, or driven to ending his own life, didn't ultimately matter.

The bourbon had proven as useful as the file, enticing enough that the pair closely watched me drinking mine, without noticing my hand dropping the powder in the bottle. I'd left them both in the closet of one of the empty rooms next to mine, wondering if anyone would find them before the hotel's busy season.

I took out my camera and shot one last image of the view down Massachusetts Avenue, while I sat on the station's steps and finished the last of the Turkish delight, the mint gel cooling the tobacco flavor in my throat.

GOODY GOOD

This, Margaret thought, was the perfect night for a walk in the forest. How fortunate that she had already agreed to be there.

Goody Price had died earlier that night, strangled by the rope as she protested her innocence and spat curses at those who sentenced her. Margaret had to laugh at the idea that people she used to think of as smart could believe anyone as dumb as the schoolteacher was a witch. Surely, a real witch could have used her powers to avoid the painful experience of hanging, or the posthumous insult of having her flesh slowly turned into nothing but burnt meat. Goody Price hadn't even been smart enough to snap her neck rather than suffocate.

Once she felt certain that she was alone, Margaret slung her bag over her shoulder and crept out to the forest on the edge of town. Nobody paid much attention to orphans, and she knew better than most how to avoid detection. It had become a particularly useful skill of late.

The noise from the woods seemed incidental when it started. Whatever it was moved through the foliage at a slow pace, but not so slowly that Margaret didn't notice it. She gave the whistle that always served as a signal, and the form in the bushes came closer. From what she could tell of its size and movement, it could have been any animal, and its eyes glowed in the darkness.

Margaret checked her surroundings, making sure she was deep enough into the forest that nobody on patrol would see her, and that none of the other children had seen her and tried to follow. "I come alone," she said, in a voice just above a whisper. "I have brought what I promised."

She whistled again, and the animal emerged from the bushes, revealing itself as a large fox. The animal's fur was red around the legs and underbelly, with silver atop its head and along its back, and a black tail ending in a white tip. The fox walked up to Margaret and sat still, wrapping its tail around its paws and scanning the forest from side to side.

"Here it is," Margaret said, reaching into the bag she'd brought, and removing several chunks of cooked meat. "I had to wait until the town watch went to bed before I could collect it." The fox's stomach rumbled when it smelled the offering, and the animal licked its chops with relish.

Margaret arranged the pieces in the usual pattern. When she finished, she looked up at the full moon and chanted the now-familiar incantation. The fox ate everything she had brought, even gnawing the marrow from what remained of Goody Price's bones. Margaret had known the schoolteacher had become suspicious of her, and the girl found relief watching the fox erase the last evidence of such suspicion. As it fed, Margaret listened for signs of any other animals that might be drawn to the scent, but the forest was completely silent. Just like the other times.

When the fox was sated, it sat on its haunches and scanned

the forest again. Then it spoke. "This task is now complete. Shall there be another task?"

Margaret nodded, and steeled herself. Even with practice, she had never lost her fear of the primeval.

"What, child, do you bring in payment?"

The girl again reached for her bag, and dumped its remaining contents on the forest floor. She had not had much time at the Price house while the town gathered at the gallows, and the late Goodman Price had not been a wealthy man. She had found a small jar of indigo, some fabric, a few apples, and a pair of candlesticks made of a shiny metal.

"This is quite a bit less than what you last offered."

The crone had taken a different form each time Margaret met with her, appearing as a marten, a wolverine, a wolf, a bat, a hawk. Somehow, Margaret found her human form most frightening, and that was the form that now picked through the scraps of the Prices' former lives.

Margaret shivered as the hunched old woman spoke. She was always careful not to make eye contact with the crone, lest her thoughts be read and controlled.

"Very well. Who shall it be this time?"

"The midwife who sometimes watches the cousins. I believe she knows too many things."

"Very well. It shall be done. You shall feed me again at the full corn moon."

Margaret nodded and lifted her face to look at her fellow conspirator, only to see a large, reddish grey weasel racing for the brush. It reminded her of the marten that approached her months ago, when she had thought she was crying in the forest by herself.

That time, the local beggar woman had seen Margaret stealing an extra share of milk, and threatened to tell everyone if she ever did it again. The scared girl ran off as soon as night fell, making sure she was alone as she entered the woods, which the town's laws forbid children from exploring. She had said "I wish I could kill Goody Good" a few times before she heard the movement in the bushes. She was terrified that someone from town had followed her, or that the noise meant she had stumbled on Naumkeag land.

Instead, she was confronted by nothing more than a marten, which calmed her. Hearing a marten say, "That can be arranged," however, was more chilling than anything the girl had feared. She hadn't fully meant what she said, but the slender animal proved persuasive. It sounded so easy, so final. Under the light of the full moon, she found herself agreeing to terms with the hag into which the marten reshaped itself.

Mere days later in town, she saw the two cousins staring into the eyes of a horned owl that had a familiar appearance. It was too late to question her decision. Though the owl didn't move its beak or produce a sound, in her head Margaret could hear the bird telling the girls that they had seen Goody Good with the devil, that the goats on which the owl had fed were killed by the old beggar woman. The girls repeated the words quietly. Soon they would repeat them to the town elders. Margaret knew the other girls would be rewarded for finding the supposed witch, but she did not need the credit.

She only needed the townspeople who were mean to her to leave her alone. One by one, she would make them.

GRANDDAD'S BALLGAME

W hen my Granddad was just a boy, to hear him tell it, there were only three things he ever wanted to do in his life.

One was to get the girl who lived on the farm catty corner to take a shine to him. Another was to see the world, or at least some part of the world outside central Indiana. The third was to make a ballplayer out of himself.

Now by the time he left school, truth be told, he hadn't made a whole lot of progress. The neighbor girl, Katie Lee, had taken to a chaste courtship with an older man, though Granddad reckoned that arrangement would prove temporary, on account of the wife everyone knew the man had back in town. The farthest Granddad had yet ventured was down to Bean Blossom for a couple of FFA get-togethers, which showed him so little of the world he deemed it statistically insignificant.

Baseball, though, that was going right nicely. He was no bona fide professional, but he could swing a bat as well as any of the boys on his local team, and played the infield a fair bit better than that. The way he figured, a baseball career could give him a leg up on his other two goals.

His own daddy felt otherwise, and used to tell him that the world needed ditch diggers too, and that there weren't anything wrong with that honest profession. Granddad didn't have much choice but to listen while under that roof, but once the consumption took his parents in the spring of forty-one, they didn't have much say in the matter, and the last ditch Granddad dug was to bury his folks on the family plot out back of the farmhouse.

Now in those days, to hear Granddad tell it, the only way to get a tryout with a real ballclub was to get your reputation known. Even bona fide professionals didn't make all that much money back then, not like it is these days. Baseball was more like a good summer job, but you still had to make your wages in the offseason. Men came home and pumped gas or worked the farm. Pick the right day, you could buy a soda from a fella who spent the summer in the big leagues. The team bosses were making their money, but...

Sorry, where was I?

So Granddad was no dummy. He knew he had the talent to stick, but every town for miles had a half dozen players as good or almost there.

Lucky for him, that winter Japan sent a mess of planes out over Pearl Harbor, and the country reacted right quick. Men his age from all over were finding themselves sent off to fight, but Granddad was four-eff on account of a fallen arch in his right foot. The country reckoned he was better used getting paid not to grow corn on the family plot, so as to keep prices from cratering, giving him plenty of time to try to practice his swing. He made a point of playing on every team that would give him a fair shake, switching teams when he had to so he could play every day, just so he might catch the eye of traveling scouts fixing to replace all the ballplayers called up to active duty. He did a lot of talking too, spreading a few tall tales among the other players, hoping something might be memorable enough to stick.

Before he could consider himself a real ballplayer, he felt like he needed a real ballplayer nickname. To Granddad, there was something romantic in the notion that a man could play one game without footwear and be known as "Shoeless Joe" for generations to come. He thought names like "Pie" Traynor or "Hippo" Vaughn were memorable enough, but he had a tiny bit of spare tire about his belly and didn't want anything that might draw questions about his figure. He liked the ring of something like Mordecai "Three-Finger" Brown, but felt a nickname that literal required a degree of sacrifice to which he couldn't quite cotton.

He told my Daddy years later that he would have liked something along the lines of old "Vinegar Bend" Mizell, if he'd been around then, until Granddad learned its origin was nothing more exciting than the name of an Alabama town near where Wilmer Mizell came into the world, and Granddad hailed from the less colorfully monikered locality of Franklin, which was his Christian name already and seemed rather redundant.

Pardon me, I'm digressing rather a bit.

Anyhow, Granddad rightly subscribed to the notion that a man can't well give himself a nickname, but he saw no reason why a man couldn't try to get one from others. So he tried his hand at leading his teammates in the direction of something suitable, trying to earn one with, what's the word, affectations. No matter how well he played, his teammates never suggested "One Sock" Wilson, or "Sleeveless Frank" Wilson, and his attempt to earn the "Eye Patch" Wilson moniker earned him nothing but a welt from an inside fastball he didn't see coming.

All through the summer of forty-two, Granddad hit like one of them metronomes, steady as they come. Teams come through town on barnstorming tours, and teams gone home talking about the shortstop from down in Franklin County. Not much power, but the man could get on base and range like a jackrabbit, though he was developing a bit of a reputation as a colorful character on account of his affectations.

Now as Granddad always told it, the first weekend in August the whole county had itself a big tournament to show off the local boys for a mess of big league scouts who were trying to fill up their minor league farm teams with some young players, on account of how many regular players were off playing on Uncle Sam's team. Mostly the whole county turned out too, and Granddad had never played ball in front of so many folks. He spied that Katie Lee was there with her daddy instead of her beau, tipped his cap to her and winked as he sprinted out to the field, but he lost her when the park kept on filling.

They didn't play the national anthem at ballgames in those days, so the crowd never really stood still while they was waiting for the game to start. By the time it did, there was so many curious folks they had to line up around the edge of the field. Granddad's squad even paid the players a little taste of the gate, on account of the bigger crowd, which in his eyes counted as making him a bona fide professional for a change.

Good thing he crossed that off his list, he used to say, as once the game against the boys from Brookville got underway, Granddad wasn't having himself much luck. Whether it were the sight of the neighbor girl, or knowing all them scouts were there, or the flashbulbs from the local news reporters, he couldn't focus himself. He wasn't alone neither; the umpire lost track of the count Granddad's first time up, but it just let him badly miss at four pitches instead of three. Next time up, he tried to pull back his swing too late and sent the ball just a few feet straight up into the air and straight back down again into the catcher's mitt.

The other players on his team fared a bit better, so Granddad looked all the worse by comparison, but the team was winning. Granddad liked to win as much as anybody, but he was no dummy, and he knew the rest of the boys looking good when he didn't wasn't going to be much use to him. Their pitcher, Lefty McCullough, was striking out so many Brookvillers that Granddad hadn't even got a chance to make a play at short.

Come the ninth inning, the fellas from Franklin was up by just one run, and McCullough's arm was starting to tire. He hit one batter, then gave up a roper that put men at the corners with two out and brought the biggest farmboy in Brookline to the plate, swinging the biggest bat most folks in the county had ever seen.

That boy hit the ball hard but low, what Granddad used to call a wormburner, a situation that shouldn't have given him much trouble. Wouldn't you know it, the ball found a pebble on its way to see Granddad, and hopped up like a grasshopper. He had to stretch to his left to corral it, and it spun him halfway round before he could make the throw to first off his back foot.

Now, any man watching would have called it a bad throw, seeing as it sailed so wide off first that old Tommy Bennett could have grown eight feet high and still not been able to reach far enough. Granddad was rightly mortified, even more so when he saw the ball heading toward the crowd, and spied a spectator moving right into its path.

Those folks who didn't see the man get hit sure did get to

hear it, seeing as the ball smacked the side of his skull and knocked him straight over like a tenpin.

The crowd, as you might expect, flocked to the spot to see just what happened, and check if the man could get his wits back about him. Even the umpire called time once there was enough commotion that the players couldn't fairly concentrate.

Now what Granddad had no way of knowing at the time was that the man he'd nearly sent to old St. Peter's doorstep was in the process of absconding with a pile of purses he'd unhelpfully collected from women as he worked his way through the stands, using a penknife to cut them straps and carefully removing the rest. When the crowd figured out the thief's plan, largely on account of the dozen handbags that fell when he did, Granddad found himself treated to proper round of applause.

To be fair, he never actually claimed he meant to hit that man and save several ladies from difficult circumstances; he just didn't see any reason to disabuse anyone of that notion. Especially when people saw fit to rush the field and lift him up on their shoulders, or when the future Katie Lee Wilson gave him a peck on the cheek on account of his rescuing her pocketbook.

They finished the game as a formality a few hours later, but, mostly, people forget the result. They remembered "Bullseye" Wilson, and people told the story of that perfectly timed throw round these parts for a long, long while.

Figuring the publicity might draw a few fans, the St. Louis Browns gave Granddad a spot on one of their farm teams, and gave him his chance to see more of America, seeing as the war kept better players otherwise occupied for a few years. As good a hitter as he was for a boy from Franklin County, he never quite measured up to the bona fide professionals, and spent most of his two summers as a ballplayer sitting on the bench. After his deal with the government as concerned his farm,

Granddad had gotten right used to drawing some money without having to do much for it, and always said he got paid to watch games from the best seats.

Now he's gone, I have to tell I never quite knew how much of Granddad's stories were monkeyshines, or how many really were truthful. To hear him tell it though, he sure did hit the bullseye on life, and there ain't no denying that.

CLARKSDALE

Milo pulled into Clarksdale just as the sun was setting. It had been a long drive from Chicago, and he had to shake his legs a bit when he first got out of the car. After grabbing his knapsack and guitar from the backseat, he handed the driver a wad of cash to cover the promised gas money and gave him a hearty handshake. He slung the bag over his shoulder, grabbed the banged-up guitar case by the handle, and walked a few blocks to the first open bar he could find.

He heard the place before he saw it. The small wooden building looked almost like a run-down garage, but the neon sign in the window promised cold beer, and the bluegrass band Milo could hear from the road knew what it was doing.

The air outside was hotter than he was used to that early in the summer, but that seemed like nothing compared to the heat once he entered the bar. In the few seconds it took him to find an empty stool for his seat and another for his stuff, the brim of his ball cap was soaked in sweat and he'd had to strip his torso down to his crusty white undershirt.

"Be right with you," called the bartender, an older man

with wiry salt-and-pepper hair and a prominent scar on the back of his neck. He was drying out a few glass mugs with a red bandana, which Milo noticed he also absentmindedly used to wipe the sweat off his brow a couple of times. Before walking over, the bartender caught a long glimpse of the band on stage, and Milo followed his eye.

The trio was still in the middle of the same extended jam that drew him to the bar in the first place, a version of "Fire on the Mountain" that seemed in no danger of ending soon. The banjo player picked better than anyone Milo had ever seen, his ebony fingers working the strings faster than seemed earthly possible. The guitarist was just as good, and the way she swayed as she played made for an exciting stage presence. The fiddler, however, was even more talented than those two. A thin man of indeterminate age, he managed to keep most of his body perfectly still while his right arm managed the bow with controlled fury, as if it had its own inclinations.

"Can I get a beer?" Milo called out, without taking his eyes off the band.

"That all depends. You got ID?" the bartender replied.

Milo made a show of searching his pockets, even though he knew he didn't have one. He'd never learned to drive, and accidentally left his state ID in a motel outside of Louisville. Sobriety had become a hazard of being baby faced.

"Tell you what, just give me a lemonade," he offered as a compromise.

"You play?" the old bartender asked, as he brought over the drink. He winked as he spiked it with a shot of something.

"Not as well as I'm going to," Milo said. "Paying a visit to the crossroads later."

The bartender let out a long whistle. "Well, you come to the right place, I guess. Where are you stayin'?"

"Nowhere in particular. Figured I'd just sleep outside. It's hot enough."

"That's sure true," the old man said. "Or you can get a room down at the Riverside. Lots of history there. Bessie Smith breathed her last in that building, and some folks still say she haunts it."

Milo nodded and sipped his lemonade. The glass was already slick with condensation, but the cold drink felt good. So good that he finished a few more while the band burned through a series of bluegrass standards.

"Why don't you break out your guitar and show us a little of what you got?" the bartender said after some time, but Milo just shook his head. Even if he didn't question his ability — and he would be miles away performing somewhere if he didn't question it — he wouldn't want to follow that trio. The heat hadn't abated either, and a good half of the bar's patrons were fanning themselves at any moment. The heat was starting to tire Milo prematurely, which combined with the alcohol to turn simply staying alert into a challenge.

A few hours and a few more drinks into the evening, the bar began to fill considerably. Nobody seemed to pay much attention to Milo, giving him a chance to listen to the band and think about the task ahead.

"You're not from around here, son," one of the other patrons said, interrupting his focus. "Where you in from?" The direct question broke Milo's focus on the band, which continued to jam on an instrumental Milo didn't recognize.

The priest was only a few years older than him, a hefty man in shirtsleeves and suspenders, his face almost glossy from sweat. He was sipping an auburn whiskey from one hand and using a paper fan to cool himself with the other. His occupation was only identifiable from the white ring around his neck, protected from the moisture by his shirt collar.

"A bit of all over," Milo told him. "Been traveling around, seeing America and all."

"Lot to see, lot to see," the priest said, stealing a glimpse at the banged-up guitar case under Milo's stool. "May I inquire as to what brings you to our little town?"

"Guess you could say Bob Johnson brought me here." He was fine with the idea of selling his soul, but for some reason still found lying to a priest too far to go.

"You know Robert died awfully young, and in a lot of pain," the priest pointed out. "You might be better off just practicing a little more. Best think about that." On the bar next to Milo, he placed a little booklet with a cross on the cover, then moved on to talk to other patrons.

Milo put the pamphlet in his jeans pocket just in case, and ordered another lemonade as the band took its bows and the full crowd applauded.

When the next group came on and launched into a bluesy version of "The House of the Rising Sun," the fiddle player took a seat at the bar next to Milo. The musician was nearly as stiff as he'd been on stage. Before he brought whiskey sours to two women dancing near the stage, he nodded at Milo's guitar and then at Milo, crossed his index fingers in an "x" shape, and winked.

It was clear early that the new band was talented, but couldn't match the previous one's musicianship. Then again, Milo noticed, where the dusk crowd was clearly there for the music, many of the latecomers were just there to find alcohol and easy sex. The musicians on stage were nicer looking and had a more populist sensibility. They encouraged the crowd to dance and sing along as they closely approximated the radio versions of blues-tinged oldies. The customers loved it, though the staff seemed to use it as an excuse to clean up and total some tabs.

Feeling like he'd been there a long time, Milo looked at the old railroad clock above the bar and saw it was already twenty minutes to midnight. "Clock's a little fast," the bartender noted. "Gives us all a hand come closing time."

Milo slipped his shirt back over his head, straightened his sweaty cap, and hurriedly gathered up his bag and his guitar.

"Before you pay ol' Lucifer, you gotta pay me first," the bartender reminded him. Milo settled the bill with cash, and politely turned down another suggestion of a place to stay. Then it was off to the spot where the devil marked his territory.

Determined to do everything right, he ignored the only driver who passed him and hiked down the road on foot, with his guitar slung over one shoulder and his knapsack of food and clothes over the other. He hiked for several minutes, following the old telephone wires, until he found the spot where Route 61 and Route 49 intersected. Looking at the sculpture of two guitars the locals had built atop the street sign, Milo thought the spot lost a bit of its mystery, like the time he hitchhiked to San Francisco and found out that the corner of Haight and Ashbury was just home to a Gap store.

The corner was quieter than he'd expected, considering midnight wasn't as late as it used to be. Though the heat was worse back in the bar, Milo still found the weather hard to bear, and he took refuge beneath a pair of short trees under the guitar sculpture. Using his packed bag as a seat, he uncased his secondhand guitar and did his best to tune it. He realized he hadn't played at all since Chicago, and the wood had reacted to the temperature. Milo picked a few songs, clumsily muting the strings with his index finger.

He had no idea how long he sat out there, and regretted trading his watch for a bus ticket in Sacramento. After he'd been practicing for a time, he set the guitar aside and knelt in the shade, letting his knees sink down into the dirt.

It was only a few seconds before he saw another soul on the road, walking toward him. The heat made everything in the distance blurry, but as the figure approached, Milo identified a man wearing a fedora and a light coat despite the temperature. He was walking an enormous wolfhound without a leash, but the hound moved in lockstep with its master. For the first time since he devised this plan, Milo felt scared, not sure what was going to happen next.

The stranger tipped his hat, and Milo recognized him as the fiddle player from the band. When he came close, the dog ran ahead and moved in front of Milo, who got up slowly so as not to startle the hound. Despite his efforts, the dog retained an unfriendly stare and gave an ongoing, low growl.

Milo was less certain about how to greet the other man and how he should explain his presence, but the fiddler seemed to already know. "May I assume you're here to make a deal?" he asked, but continued before Milo had a chance to answer. "Let me see the guitar."

Careful not to brush it against his dirt-stained jeans, Milo handed over his guitar, having to pass it over the intractable hound. Milo watched transfixed as the fiddler fiddled with the strings, tuning each in a matter of seconds and fingering the fretboard with lightning speed.

Pointing at Milo with a long finger, he said, "Call the tune." The first song that popped in his head was "Crawdad," and the hound made sure he stayed in place while listening. Milo had never heard anyone play it so well or so fast, and the idea of doing that himself excited him more than he expected.

When the song was over, the fiddler handed the guitar back to Milo. It felt unusually hot to the touch, though Milo questioned how much of that could be blamed on the weather and how much on the furious playing it had just endured. He had to blow on it a few times before his fingertips didn't smart from contact.

"How do I...well, I guess how do I pay you?" Milo asked, bracing himself for what was to come.

"Our dealings are already complete," the fiddler said. "Business was all done before we spoke. Now, it wouldn't be fair if I didn't remind you that you'll have to play that guitar often if you still want it to play like that, and the more you practice with it, the better it'll sound."

"But—"

"But nothing. You think Mr. Bob just walked away from the crossroads an overnight virtuoso? He played and played, kept that fire alive in him."

Milo had somehow thought Clarksdale would provide an alternative to practice, but his mother always told him to understand a deal before agreeing, and he knew there was no point in arguing. He'd already come to terms just by hitching down there. With the hound watching him closely, he carefully laid his guitar back in its case.

"Another thing before I forget," the fiddler said. "Nobody thought too much of Bob when he was alive. The legend grows over time. Don't be surprised if the crowds you play for don't react the way you want. They may not hear it."

With that, the fiddler tipped his hat and started to walk back down the road. After a few paces, he snapped his fingers and the hound turned to follow. Before Milo could fully process his thoughts, the pair had disappeared into the night.

Not sure how much time had passed, Milo walked down the road in the opposite direction. When he found a bench, he settled in with his knapsack as a pillow and his arms holding the guitar to his chest. He expected to have trouble sleeping, but the heat made him groggy, and he was asleep within minutes.

The next morning, the young musician stood along the side of Route 61 with his right thumb out, his cap backward and the guitar case in his left hand. Milo decided he'd try to get to Muscle Shoals. Maybe he'd try for a steady gig at a roadhouse there, or test his playing a bit and move on to Nashville or Memphis. Maybe he'd get some recognition before he found a hellhound on his trail.

In a diner across the road, the fiddler and the priest from the bar shared a laugh over grits and waffles, thinking about how many young musicians had come and gone in the same fashion and wondering how many still thought they'd traded one kind of soul for another. Some visitor had told them years ago that the devil's greatest trick was making the world believe he didn't exist, but they believed the church's was making sure people still believed he did.

The priest ordered them each a sweet tea as the fiddler pulled out a chess set. It was still too hot out to do much else.

THE ORACLE'S CURSE

Just five seconds earlier, she had seemed too good to be true. He should have known there was something a little off, just waiting to reveal itself.

"Come on, it'll be fun. I'll pay for it," Karyn said while the two of them waited for their dessert.

"You don't really believe in all that?" Larry replied, trying to hedge his tone between faux worry and gentle kidding. "Do you?"

Larry Pemberton really liked this girl. As a guy who always had standards a little too high for his side of the ledger, he didn't meet many women he wanted to see the socially accepted three times. Through two dates, Karyn had seemed like a good match. She was smart, accomplished, beautiful...And, it turned out, a believer in mystical powers.

"It depends," she said, interrupting his skeptical thoughts. "You have to go to the right one, obviously. A lot of them are just making things up, or telling you what they think you want to hear..."

The concept of a "right" psychic was a concept Larry

found pretty silly. He'd thought so even when he was a little kid watching television with his mother on days he was too sick to go to school. One of the daytime talk shows she used to regularly watch would sometimes feature a "celebrity" psychic named Priscilla. Larry must have been home sick for a disproportionate number of her appearances because — despite his mother's claims that the show usually promoted authors and actors a young boy would find more interesting than a withered woman in a kaftan — Priscilla seemed to show up almost exactly as often as his childhood colds.

"The first time I went was when my friend Monica thought her boyfriend was cheating on her," Karyn continued. "She only had to ask her a couple of questions..."

Thinking about Priscilla for the first time in years, Larry never really understood why certain psychics broke through as celebrities. Priscilla certainly didn't do so based on her predictions, which somehow managed to be wrong even with all the vague language she used to hedge against making a definitive call. He couldn't help but think of some of his favorite examples. One year, she predicted repeatedly that the Detroit Tigers would win the championship, only they lost in the World Series to the Cardinals; Priscilla insisted her second sight didn't necessarily mean the world championship, and that the American League title qualified. That did provide the saving grace of getting Larry's mother to stop watching her appearances; Mr. Pemberton had put a pretty significant bet on the Tigers. Even Priscilla's verbal gymnastics to explain her 2000 election predictions hadn't accomplished that.

"A lot of people thought it was obvious, but Monica knew as soon as Ms. Aurelia..."

The worst example Larry could remember happened when he was in high school, though it involved a different psychic. When one of his classmates had disappeared for three weeks, the desperate suburban police department struggled to find leads, and hired a local woman who advertised her medium services on bus benches and in the free coupon flier from the grocery store. The move got a lot of local attention, and the psychic's bloody visions of what had happened to the girl would have made a pretty good plot for a crime novel. The only flaw was that Larry's classmate turned up a few weeks later, very much alive and not at all dismembered, after hitching a ride back from a trip to follow Phish around the Pacific Northwest without parental permission.

"I'm just saying there's no way you can know if you've never tried it. I never did until college…"

Karyn mentioning college reminded Larry that the girl sitting across from him had gone to the University of Chicago. With a master's in political science. That she was now a prominent fellow at a think tank on economic policy. She was a lot smarter than him in most ways. Then again, he read once that Arthur Conan Doyle believed in fairies, and Larry personally knew his share of otherwise wise people who still feared the devil literally.

"Besides, it's not like I'd ever ask her anything important. Usually she just reassures me if I'm on the right track or has some pretty obvious advice. I guess sometimes it's comforting to hear it from a stranger."

"Well, I guess I don't see any harm in that," Larry said.

"Maybe it could be fun. We'll go on the way home, I promise."

This eased his mind a little. He really did like this girl. She could have suggested trying just about anything short of ritual animal sacrifice and he would have agreed to give it a try. Plus, it closed the subject for now and let him shift the conversation back to more comfortable territory.

After they finished their profiteroles and paid the bill,

Larry got their jackets from the coat check, and they started to walk up Clark Street. He felt he'd picked a perfect night for a long stroll, with the temperature just cool enough to justify jackets but just warm enough for them to enjoy the walk. It wound up not mattering much, as they'd barely walked three blocks before Karyn pointed out the address of the psychic she wanted to visit.

If Larry hadn't been skeptical already, he would have been as soon as he learned that this supposedly brilliant seer advertised with a short plastic sandwich board placed in front of a mechanic's garage that had already closed for the night. The cheap letter decals spelled:

Miss Aurelia

Psycic

She Knows ALL You're Secrets

Open 5-10

The letters were accompanied by a few cone-shaped wizard hats, crescent moons, and stars. Larry checked the time on his cell phone, hoping dinner had run later than he'd thought. It was only 9:32.

"The grammatical errors don't exactly inspire confidence," Larry said.

"Okay, smart guy," Karyn replied, giving him a playful punch in the shoulder. "Just show me you can be flexible on this, and maybe I'll show you how flexible I can be, if you catch my meaning." As she said it, she twirled her hair in just the right way, knowing she'd just won that argument. Larry smiled as Karyn rang the doorbell and a loud buzzing sound indicated they could enter.

Miss Aurelia's door opened to a narrow flight of stairs that led up to what was obviously a pair of residences. The one on the right side had a welcome mat in front and children's hand-made Halloween decorations hung below the brass knocker. The one on the left of the stairs had a frame surrounded by chasing lights, and a huge sign reading "Miss Aurelia. Enter and Learn All." Larry couldn't help but wonder how often the poor family across the hall had to contend with Aurelia's customers banging on their door.

"Come in," a voice called when Karyn rapped gently on the psychic's door, and the pair entered what struck Larry as the unfortunate result of a major sale at the local head shop. Miss Aurelia had turned her kitchen into a makeshift waiting room, with a pair of upholstered benches and a table full of old magazines positioned next to the front door. The kitchen walls were covered with a patchwork of glow-in-the-dark moon and star decals, and the overhead light fixture had some kind of gel inside that bathed the whole room in a green tint that Larry assumed was meant to be eerie. A few framed photos of specific tarot cards covered the kitchen cabinets, and the round table in the center had a series of card decks in various states of stacking. It also held a half-filled ashtray, the scent of which the various incense burners around the room weren't masking as well as Miss Aurelia seemed to hope they would.

Then there was Miss Aurelia herself, who entered the kitchen through a curtain of multicolored glass beads. The accent of the voice that told them to come in sounded like some kind of Creole, with a hint of Caribbean inflection thrown in, but Larry could tell right away that it was an affectation. The woman who greeted them was a ruddy-faced Caucasian woman of about sixty, with a damp mass of unkempt red hair and a pudgy figure like that of a grandmother in a child's story-book. She wore an oversized dress that could have been either a large dashiki or a hippie's maternity wear, and a pair of thick-framed glasses that made her appearance even more comical than her accent.

"Karyn, my chile, how are ya?" the psychic cooed as they hugged, and then turned to shake Larry's hand. "And dis must be ya new man."

"That's some impressive deduction right there," Larry said, careful to make it sound like a joke, even as the older woman gave him a sideways glance.

"Will ya be wantin' one reading together, or one each?" Miss Aurelia asked. As she spoke, she was wrapping her hair in a white bath towel, making Larry wonder if it was supposed to look like a turban on a cartoon mystic or if their arrival had interrupted her shower.

"One each," Karyn said, as she reached into her purse and pulled out a pair of twenties. Larry made a motion to pay, but she waved him off and reminded him that it was her idea and she'd offered to pay.

"Who first?" the psychic asked. She lit a clove cigarette, and the smoke caused Larry to cough, as years of living in a city with no indoor smoking had made his lungs lose their immunity to it.

"First-timers first," Karyn said, gently pushing Larry forward between his shoulder blades.

Miss Aurelia stubbed out her cigarette in the ashtray in a silent gesture of accommodation, but not without a grudging eye roll in Larry's direction. "Dis way," she said, leading Larry through the beaded curtain and down a hallway into a room that was designed to serve as a guest bedroom, but which was decorated in the same garish style as the kitchen. They sat on plastic chairs on opposite sides of a card table, as the psychic began shuffling a deck of tarot cards.

"I apologize," she said. "Do ya want da tarot? I can also read ya cards from da I Ching, or read your lifelines."

"They're all just as accurate, huh?" Larry said, no longer trying to mask his sarcasm now that Karyn was several rooms away.

"Ah, I can see ya da not believe in da power," she said. "How da ya want me to prove it to ya?"

"You can start by dropping the phony accent," Larry said. "If you really have psychic powers, you can tell me all about it in your regular voice."

"Oh good," Miss Aurelia said, instantly taking the lilt out of her voice and letting her accent revert to a standard Midwestern one. "The accent's hard to keep up sometimes, but I like to give customers the full experience. It adds to the whole sense of intrigue and mystery, don't you agree?"

"That's all it took to get you to admit this whole thing is fake?"

"No, I think you misunderstand," she said, choosing the I Ching deck and shuffling it instead of the tarot. "The power is absolutely real. People just don't get as excited hearing it in my real voice. One of my mentors said I sounded too much like everyone's high school English teacher."

"Well, my high school English teacher was an old man with an Irish brogue..."

"Your sarcasm is noted, sir. Okay? But your girlfriend paid for a reading, and I don't plan to take her money without giving you an accurate one. I'm already shuffling your cards. I want you to clear your mind and focus on one question, anything you want answered. Once it's in your head, I want you to tell me to stop shuffling three times, and the cards I land on will tell you the answer to your question."

Not wanting to leave Karyn alone in the waiting room too long, Larry stopped arguing and went ahead with his reading. He didn't think of any particular question. He just stopped the shuffling at three random intervals and watched Miss Aurelia spread the three cards in front of her, as she explained that every combination of three cards made up a hexagram.

"I can count to six," Larry said, urging her on with his hand. "So what does it say?"

"You've chosen oppressed, a tree surrounded by walls," she said, pointing to the rows of broken and unbroken lines formed by the cards. "It means 'Confined, creating success. Constancy of a great person, good fortune. Not a mistake. There are words, not trusted.' Does that answer your question?"

"I don't trust these words that you're saying. Is that what it's supposed to mean? I'm right?"

"It means it answers your question. Only you know how the answer fits."

"So in other words, it's purposefully vague b.s. that anyone can twist into any answer they want."

"Fine. What will it take to convince you?"

"Something concrete. Something that can be proven right or wrong. Tell me something about me that you couldn't possibly know."

"Okay. You really like the woman out there."

"You don't need to be a psychic to see that. I'm pretty sure the waiter at dinner figured that one out."

"Your name is Larry. You're a professional, probably a lawyer..."

"She told you the first part, and this suit makes the second part a pretty obvious guess."

"You don't believe in anything you can't prove."

"Me and most people."

She paused in thought briefly. "Ah, I think I know how to prove it to you."

"Yeah?" Larry was quickly tiring of this exchange.

"I am going to put a curse on you, one that will have real consequences for your future."

"Right. That I'd like to see. Go right ahead."

"So be it."

With that, Miss Aurelia clapped twice and the lights in the room all turned off, except for the row of black-light lamps on the back wall. She stood and leaned back, with her hands raised toward the ceiling. Tilting her head up, the psychic began to rant in what was either a language Larry didn't recognize or gibberish designed to sound like that. Then she leaned forward with both arms outstretched and pointed at Larry.

"I curse you, Mr. Larry! As a direct result of this meeting tonight, misfortune will befall you, and you will question the way you reacted to me! With all my powers, I assure it!" She didn't yell it, but said it with a hard edge of anger in her voice. She stayed locked on Larry, thrashing her arms at him for a few seconds, then leaned back again. When she sat down and clapped for the lights to return, she instantly reverted to her previous, bemused-but-polite demeanor.

"Wow, that was really scary," Larry said. "Guess I'm cursed now. Better make sure I don't walk under a ladder on my way home."

"Just remember that I told you so," Miss Aurelia said as she walked to the door and led him back toward the kitchen. "You'll soon encounter your misfortune."

"Sure," Larry said as they passed through the beaded curtain and back to where Karyn was sitting on one of the benches, leafing through a two-year-old issue of a new age magazine Larry had never seen before.

"How did it go?" Karyn asked as she stood up, giving Larry half a hug. "Told you it would be fun."

"Yeah, it was really fun," Larry said, sounding sincere this time. "I guess you were right again."

"Come chile, it's ya turn," Miss Aurelia said, immediately

regaining her faux accent. She gave Larry a dirty look before smiling at Karyn and leading her back to the reading room.

While Karyn got her reading, Larry sat on the bench thumbing through magazines before settling on some decade-old *National Geographic* issues to admire the photography. He couldn't tell if Karyn's reading was taking substantially longer than his, or if it just felt that way because of his boredom and the oppressive smell of contradictory incense blending.

When Karyn eventually emerged through the beads, without the psychic, Larry asked how the reading went.

"Good," she said. "She answered some important questions."

"I'll bet. Ready to head back?"

He walked Karyn another few blocks north to her apartment, again thankful for the weather. Larry made a few light jokes about some of the psychic's specific guesses, like the shocking observation that he was into the girl he was dating. Karyn laughed, and Larry thought it wasn't worth bringing up the alleged curse. He wasn't worried about it, but he also didn't want to freak her out, knowing she actually believed in some of this hokum.

"This is me," she said when they got to the front stoop of her brownstone. "Thank you very much for dinner, and for coming with me to Miss Aurelia's."

She didn't make any motion to kiss him, and the lack of an invitation to come upstairs left Larry standing there awkwardly, unsure of what to say.

"Um, is there something else you'd like to do?" he tried, hoping to break the tension. "Maybe get a nightcap?"

"No, I don't think so," Karyn said, shifting nervously. "The thing is, well, I don't think we should see each other anymore."

"What? Did I do something..."

"It was something Miss Aurelia said. She told me you have

a dark aura that can only bring bad things to me. I know you don't really believe in it, but she's never steered me badly when it comes to relationships..."

Larry tried to protest, but after a few minutes it was clear nothing he said was getting through. He stopped listening closely as she explained further, gave him a short and unemotional hug, and went up her front steps. He tried to gather his thoughts before he turned around and headed back to where he'd parked his car in front of the restaurant.

As a dejected Larry walked back to retrieve his car, he again saw the psychic's plastic sandwich board in front of her place. When he looked up, he saw her watching him from her open window above the mechanic's garage, and smelled the clove cigarette she was smoking. She wasn't wearing the turban or the oversized glasses anymore, but she did wear a sly smile on her face.

"Hey Mr. Larry," she called down. When he looked up, she pointed directly at him, and yelled, "Told you so, you silly man. You should not have doubted the power." With that, she slammed the window and closed the curtains.

Larry again stood awkwardly for a few seconds, trying to gather his thoughts. Then he went to recover his car and drive home alone, but not before kicking over her sandwich board and jumping on it a few times.

CROCOTTA

Study the unexplainable long enough, and you'll learn there's usually an explanation.

The gryphon? Just protoceratops bones, discovered by Proto-Greeks who didn't understand what they were seeing. The centaur? Horse archers of the Eurasian steppe, so adept on their steeds that they seemed to merge into one being. The roc, a bird big enough to carry elephants in its claws? Just the bones of bird-hipped dinosaurs with elephantine claws.

The crocotta, however, is real. I promise.

When I arrived here three years ago, looking to learn more about the animal, I was of the opinion it was just a case of the ancient Romans having never seen a hyena before and exaggerating its size the way they did their opponents' armies. When the locals would tell me the crocotta could change from male to female at will, I explained that hyenas are one of the few animal species in which males and females look alike. When they told me that the crocotta called out names in the night, I talked about the strange pitch of the hyena's voice and how it can sound human.

I believed everything I said, and never questioned it. Until Joseph.

One night, a few weeks after I arrived, he returned home from his job at the local fruit market. According to his teenage daughter, he made dinner for the two of them, then sat up reading a book until he heard someone calling his name. Marie said she didn't recognize the voice, and that it said nothing except Joseph's name, every few minutes, in a pitch so clear that it sounded like the speaker was inside their small home. Her father told her to go to bed, and not to worry about what she heard. When she woke up to use the toilet a few hours later, Joseph was gone. She could see from the window that he had left town and was walking into the forest.

He never came back. By the next morning, it seemed the whole town was convinced that the crocotta had called him to his death and eaten him alive. A few men followed his footprints to the edge of the forest, but they were too scared to go in.

The next several weeks were quiet, and I tried to assure everyone that it had just been a coincidence, that there had to be a rational explanation for why Joseph went into the forest. An old beggar woman refused to believe me, insisting the man had been eaten alive, and that he was just one of many. She brought me little balls of coarse fur that she claimed the crocotta left on the forest floor, but they felt like they could have come from a dog, or even a wild cat. She warned that the quiet period only meant the monster's appetite had been satisfied, and that it would hunt again.

A few months later, a man I never met left home unannounced, and the rumors swirled again.

Then a young girl.

I tried organizing a party to search the woods and find evidence of what had happened, but most people were too terrified to help. I started to notice that calm actually birthed their fear; the disappearances were almost welcomed, with relief it wasn't them. When the beggar woman went missing, nobody even claimed to hear the crocotta call her, as she had nobody around to fear for her.

Months went by before Marie heard her name. I was with her at the time, as she had agreed to accompany me to the woods for a search, so I heard it too. The voice was hard to distinguish, neither male nor female, but somehow both. It just said her name, calmly but forcefully, and I've never seen anyone as afraid as Marie was when she heard it. She froze in place, and looked at me to see if I'd heard the same thing. When I nodded, she began to run back the way we came, yelling for me to follow.

I ran after her, but she was younger and more athletic, and I wasn't able to catch up. I lost sight of her until I stopped to catch my breath. There was a noise far behind me, and though I turned expecting to see an animal, I saw Marie walking in the wrong direction, back into the forest, as if in a trance. She didn't answer when I yelled her name, nor did she even seem to hear me, so I followed her as well as I could. Still unable to gain ground, the last thing I saw was the shadow of the beast's gaping maw, and the last thing I heard was a sound of crushed bone. Marie never screamed or yelled for help.

Thinking there might still be time, I ran to the spot, but the only sign that she had ever been there was a line of her foot-prints in the mud, and a similar line of prints like a dog's, but they had to come from a dog larger than any I've ever heard about. Once I gave up hope of finding the girl alive, I searched for fur, scat, anything to take back and analyze. I didn't find anything, but I felt like something was watching my progress from the thicket.

When I told people in town what had happened, I mostly

received recriminations about why I didn't believe them before. Nobody seemed to think I should have been able to save the girl, or wondered why I couldn't find proof of what happened. Only I questioned what I had seen, and came to believe the voice in the night that terrified ancient peoples, from Ethiopia to Rome to India, had belonged to something more sinister than a scavenging hyena.

I tell you all this because I heard the crocotta's voice again tonight.

This time, it was calling my name.

THE CAT

Sitting in a bar on Christmas Eve didn't feel out of the ordinary for David Silver. He was still unmarried, and his last relationship had ended months earlier, before there was even an awkward discussion about whose parents they would visit and how much time he'd need to take off work and what was an appropriate amount to spend on gifts. He was an only child, and had come to an agreement with his parents to take a trip to Vegas together in the spring rather than have him spend an exorbitant amount and battle transit stress to fly to Minneapolis for a few days just because the calendar suggested it.

That it was Christmas Eve was largely immaterial to him, since he hung out at the same bar nearly every night anyway. David couldn't cook worth anything, and it was too cold this time of year to walk to a decent carryout place when the Ceilidh Moon Bar and Grill was located literally forty paces from the front door of his old apartment building, the kitchen was usually open until four, and the tater tots reminded him of the ones his mother fried up when he was little. He would have been sitting there, eating tots and drinking a pint of lager in his usual seat at one end of the curved bar, if it was almost any other Tuesday.

On top of all that, he wasn't even Christian.

The one thing out of the ordinary on Christmas Eve was the crowd. The Ceilidh Moon was the kind of place that didn't stand out in a neighborhood with more than two dozen bars. The crowd most nights consisted mostly of patrons who, while not necessarily regulars, were definitely locals. Couples who'd stop in for a quick bite, guys who would sit at the bar and banter with the bartenders about their day, second shifters taking advantage of their one chance to socialize. Most nights, the jukebox output fit the decor, with the voices of Ronnie Drew or Shane MacGowan mixing with the same kinds of strings, drums, accordions, and whistles placed on shelves throughout the establishment. The mood was usually upbeat, but in an everyday, hail-fellow-well-met manner.

This night was different.

For one thing, there were a lot more people. David wasn't eavesdropping, but he overheard enough to know at least a few of the bigger groups were made up of high school classmates in town for the holiday, meeting as a way of collectively avoiding family obligations until the next day while ostensibly catching up on the last year. There were more drunks than usual, mostly sad-sack types consuming hard liquor by themselves at the bar, either trying to overcompensate for feeling all alone or trying to forget the people who made them wish they were all alone. The Irish couple who owned the bar and usually served the drinks themselves had taken the night off, leaving the job in the hands of an eager young man and an unsmiling woman back home between semesters of law school, and letting them close at midnight. Even the music was different, as the more transient customers had spent their quarters on seasonal staples by Bobby Helms and Eartha Kitt and Burl Ives.

There was also a cat.

The cat was directly opposite David, seated on the top of the bar. The very idea of a cat in the Ceilidh Moon was striking and rather weird, but this was also a rather strikingly weird cat. It had the look of a house cat, but was significantly bigger than any he'd ever seen, closer in magnitude to a small dog. David assumed from the cat's size that it was a he, and he was a mostly black cat with a large, white patch on his chest. The cat sat upright with his front paws touching, and his back paws perfectly aligned alongside them, sitting so still that he could have been a statue if not for the green eyes scanning the room on high alert.

"Any idea where the cat came from?" David turned to ask the people sitting next to him, only to find that the two frat guys who had been there a few minutes earlier were now occupied in a darts game, and that both bartenders were in back. David took another sip from his lager and went back to writing some work ideas on a small notepad. Still, he kept looking across the bar at the cat, who now seemed to be staring specifically at him.

By the time the bartender returned with his sandwich and another drink, David had grown bored and started a sketch of the cat on his notepad, figuring the animal's stillness and focus made it a perfect model. The younger man, whose name tag identified him as Colin, hadn't seemed to notice the animal's presence until David asked him, "Do you know what the deal is with the cat?"

"No idea. It can't be the boss's cat; he's allergic. Where'd he come from?"

"Couldn't tell you. I just turned around and he was sitting there."

"Heh. It looks like he's waiting to order. Like he thinks he's people."

"He definitely looks like he's waiting for something," David said. "You could at least give him some milk."

David had been joking, but the bartender took out the cream kept on hand for White Russians and poured some of it into a coffee cup. As he placed it in front of the cat, the animal didn't appear at all skittish, though he watched Colin intently until the transaction was complete. David could have sworn the cat looked across the bar at him and nodded before starting to lap up the cream with his pink tongue.

After watching the animal drink for a bit, David returned to his sketch as the music switched over to Greg Lake professing his belief in Christmas stories. He was nearly finished drawing, and was starting to feel a slight buzz from his beverage, when the jukebox began playing an old chestnut about said nuts roasting on an open fire. He started to hum along, and noticed someone else was humming in the seat next to him.

"That's a good drawing," said the stout older man, who had sat down without David noticing. "I take it you like cats?"

"Yes. I only have one now, but I've always had cats."

"Good for you. A lot of people say they're afraid of them."

"My great-grandmother was like that. She had a lot of superstitions from the old country."

"What old country? What superstitions?" the stranger said. "I'm sorry if I seem nosy. I'm just curious about these kinds of things."

"No, it's fine. She grew up in a rural part of Ireland where almost everyone believed in stuff like that. She showed me where it was on a map once, but I don't remember the name. It wasn't really near Cork, but it was closer to Cork than to any other city, if that makes sense."

"Sure."

"She used to complain because my mother would let our cat in the room when I was a baby. She used to think cats would steal children's souls while they slept."

"Do you think she really believed that?"

"Definitely," David said, thinking about his long-dead great-grandmother for the first time in years. "When she got sick, she stayed with us for a few months, and she used to lock our cat Tommy in the basement. I could play with him down there, but she wouldn't let him follow us upstairs. He was the sweetest cat you'd ever meet, and she was absolutely terrified of him."

"I've never understood how people could be that afraid of cats." The stranger scratched his beard, but otherwise gave David his full attention. "They've always been perfectly friendly to me."

"It wasn't just cats; she was superstitious about a lot of things," David said, surprising himself with how much he remembered. "My mother told me a story once about going to a farm with her. My mother was young, I think twelve or thirteen, and was dying to learn how to ride a horse. So she talked her grandmother into taking her to a farm that had a stable. They drove two hours to get there, and then turned right around. She wouldn't let my mother learn to ride because the stable only had black horses, and she thought one of them might be a pooka who would carry her off."

"Strange, that. I will say, you seem like you don't believe any of this stuff." The stranger signaled to the female bartender, pointing to David's glass to get him a refill, but without ordering anything for himself.

"I'm not much for believing in mythology. I am sitting in a bar on Christmas Eve."

"Surely you know that this day had nothing to do with

Christianity," the man said. "I don't mean to offend you, but the Christians only used this day to co-opt the winter solstice. A day that belonged to those who came long before them..."

"I know all that, and no offense taken. I'm not Christian. I mean, my great-grandmother was, but she was the only one on that side of the family."

David did worry that the stranger might be offending some of the other customers as the man continued to explain the pagan origins of the holiday, how there were and had always been metaphysical forces in the world that animals understand better than people, and how people like his great-grandmother were more in tune than others but didn't really understand the world. One couple talking nearby left in an unmistakable huff when the man pointed to the bar's Christmas tree next to the fireplace and called it a "particularly clever way of associating their god with the ancient symbol of everlasting life."

By the time this history lesson was complete, David had finished the last of his food and the fresh drink that arrived. When he was done talking, the stranger stood up to leave. "Thanks for listening to me," the man said, patting David on the shoulder. He started to walk away, but turned just long enough to say, "Before I forget, when you see O'Toole, tell him that O'Flaherty is dead."

"I don't know who you mean..." David replied, but the stranger was beyond hearing range, and David didn't see any reason to chase him down. Instead, he went back to his drawing of the cat. When he looked across the bar to use his model, however, he found the animal had left that spot and the bowl of cream had been licked clean. David continued his sketch from memory, as best he could, listening to one Christmas song after another as the crowd gradually faded. The buzz he'd acquired from his drinks faded a bit less quickly. He paid his check as soon as the younger bartender announced last call at midnight, leaving a generous holiday tip.

As the jukebox played Shane and Kirsty singing about the boys of the NYPD choir, David Silver donned his coat and scarf and headed out of the Ceilidh Moon in the early minutes of what had become Christmas Day.

* * *

Snow was falling when David left the bar, but the night was actually pleasant. There wasn't enough to please anyone dreaming of an alabaster holiday, and the lack of wind mixed with his alcohol consumption made the midnight air feel warmer than a thermometer would admit. Warm enough that he decided to walk off what remained of his modest intoxication and pick up a few supplies from the all-night convenience store at the other end of the block. The weather report had predicted a substantial storm coming the following night, and he thought it couldn't hurt to be prepared.

David Silver walked to the end of the street, listening to the sounds made by the bar's emptying of the night's last patrons and by a few cars vacating the area as their owners shifted to holiday preparation. In just the time it took him to cover a block, the night had gone silent. Except for one thing. As he passed the alley between the furniture shop and the bookstore, he heard a loud rustling. Turning to look, he could see something was moving in the middle of a pile of trash bags stacked next to an overfilled dumpster. Almost as soon as he turned, a shape emerged from under the pile and sprang out of the alley in David's direction.

Another cat.

This one looked a lot like the one he'd seen in the bar, but also different enough that nobody paying attention would ever confuse them for the same individual. This cat was also black, with the same kind of white spot on its chest, though the spot was a little larger and more oblong. The animal was shaped differently than the one he'd seen in the Ceilidh Moon, long and lean where the other was bulky. Still closer to the size of a dog than of a typical cat, but more like a small greyhound in build.

Though it darted toward David, the animal stopped abruptly just a few inches from his feet. After his conversation at the bar, David couldn't help but laugh, thinking about how pleased his great-grandmother would have been that he avoided the cat crossing his path. He had yet to encounter a cat-related superstition she hadn't fervently believed and warned him about in the few years their lives intersected.

This cat was also in considerably worse condition than the other one. Its fur was patchy, with some sections appearing sticky or mussed, and others missing as if lost in a fight with other animals. The left ear was missing the tip, and the mostly black fur had a few streaks of grey. The cat's battle scars weren't fresh, just signs that the feline had probably used up a few of its allegedly recurring lives.

"Hi there, little one," David said, in the tone of voice he unconsciously reserved for babies and fuzzy animals. "Where'd you come from?" The cat treated the question rhetorically, simply tilting its head and not even giving him a meow. It didn't try to rub up against him the way cats usually did, but it didn't flee either; it just sat still and silently regarded him. When David reached down to pet it, the cat reared its head just out of his reach, but the rest of its body stayed in place.

David left the animal where it sat, passed the furniture store and went inside the little bodega, which was empty except for a teenage clerk reading a sports magazine and watching stop-motion Christmas cartoons on a small television set. David said good evening and received a mumbled response, then began his impulse-driven shopping for the next few days. A loaf of bread, a half gallon of milk, a block of Colby cheese, a bag of chips. He went back and forth on whether he had paper towels and bar soap in his place, and was equally indecisive about whether he really needed a pint of ice cream, before throwing all those items in his handheld basket. Passing the pet food, he was sure he had more than enough on hand for his own cat, but grabbed one can for the hungry one outside, guessing the tuna flavor was the most universally beloved. The teenager said little as he scanned David's groceries and arranged them in a large paper bag. David swiped his credit card and wished the clerk a mere goodnight, then corrected himself and added a happy but unspecific holiday.

The snowfall was lighter when he returned to the outdoors, and David couldn't help but catch a few flakes with his tongue. The ground around him featured a light and mostly unspoiled dusting, in which he saw the absent cat's oversized paw prints leading away from where David last saw it and back toward the alley. When David got to the alley, he took the can of food from the bag and pulled back the ring on top, knowing from experience that the slow scratch of an opening tin was usually an automatic draw for cats.

"Here, little one," he said as he entered the alley. "I've got something for you."

"For me?" a voice replied. David realized there was a gaunt, homeless woman sitting near the dumpster. He couldn't have guessed her age, with her skin and hair showing heavy damage that could just as easily be from stress or the elements as time. "I appreciate the thought, sir, but we don't all actually have to eat cat food. Tell you the truth, the restaurants around here throw out a lot of perfectly good food."

"Oh, I'm so sorry, I didn't mean it like that," David said,

putting the half-open can back in his bag. "I just didn't see you there."

"Sir, if I've learned anything from life on the streets, it's that most people are experts at not seeing things that are sitting right in front of them. Especially if they're inconvenient to see."

"Please, I didn't mean it that way. I just bought this for a cat I saw around here. Really thin, but with a big frame. Black with a white spot."

"I know the cat you're talking about. You could say she lives here with me."

"Is she your cat?"

The woman laughed at that, but it was a wheezy kind that only lasted half a second. "As much as such a thing is possible. We can no more own a cat than we can the wind or the rain. A man can own a dog; that's as easy as owning a table. Or a horse. A man can even own a donkey, though the beast outlives him more often than not. A cat is different. Don't you agree?"

"I don't know. I've had my cat Beauregard for almost nine years, and I raised him from an orphan."

"See, the cat sounds like your ward. You care for him, you feed him, I assume you love him, and he probably loves you as well. But he's no more your possession than you are his."

"It sounds like you've thought about this a lot." This was the longest conversation David had ever had with a homeless person before money was requested, though he'd already decided to give her the four bucks he had left in his wallet whenever their conversation wrapped.

"Look around, sir. I have plenty of time and space to think about things these days. Now, you could call the cat you saw earlier my traveling companion. Do you know the old story of Dick Whittington?"

"I think so. The guy who went to London because the streets were paved with gold, and he traveled with a cat..."

"The streets in the real world are rarely paved with gold, sir, and it can be a long way down from where we started life. Trust me. But a loyal cat always makes for good company on the journey. Don't you agree?"

"Sure. Does this cat have others like her that hang out in the alley? I saw one earlier tonight that could be her brother, only he was a lot bigger." David left out anything about that cat's superior condition, but he was curious if there was an explanation for his random sightings of similar felines. The woman didn't say anything, but shook her head. "What's the cat's name? I hate to just keep calling it 'the cat.'"

"Cats have their own names that aren't for humans to know. We name them for our own benefit, but they will always know the names they're born with." She continued to pontificate on how those who came before understood this better, how the ancient Egyptians and the ancient Celts had held cats in the proper esteem, and how the modern world and its conveniences were replacing this deep connection.

She went on like this for a few minutes, obviously glad to have someone listening. David couldn't quite tell if he was listening to a smart woman who had trouble organizing her thoughts out loud after whatever misfortunes had befallen her, or a harmless but ultimately crazy woman who would be a cat hoarder if she had a permanent residence in which to hoard them.

David didn't want to be rude, but the hour was catching up to him and he was starting to tire of this chat. He gave what he hoped was a realistic yawn, which did interrupt the woman's train of thought. "It's getting late, I think I need to get going," he said, careful to avoid using the word "home" or anything else that might cause offense.

"A new king is born today," the old woman said. It was the first succinct sentence she'd said in a while.

"It is Christmas Day, isn't it? Well, merry Christmas to you..."

"No, the real king, of those who came long before. Do you know what this day really means?"

Rather than sit through another long lecture like the one he'd received at the bar, David just nodded. "Yes, the celebration of the winter solstice."

"More than that, today. More than that..." The woman suddenly stood up and stumbled closer to him, her voice growing more urgent. "O'Flaherty is dead. You must tell O'Toole."

"I will if I see him," David replied, knowing nothing about what that meant but at least knowing it meant his two random encounters weren't entirely random. "Here, before I forget." He placed his grocery bag on the ground, and found the partially opened tin of cat food. He gave it to the woman, along with his bag of chips. He started to reach for his wallet, but she shook her head and told him the food was all she required.

As he left the alley and started walking home, David Silver paused a few times to look for fresh cat tracks in the fallen snow, but discovered that even the ones he'd seen earlier were now covered by a soft layer of virgin powder. Only his own footprints remained.

* * *

A few minutes later, David Silver was walking up the backstairs to his second-floor apartment. His arm had gotten tired from carrying the bag of groceries, so he placed it down on the wood railing while he searched his pocket for his keys. Once found, the keys dropped from his hands, and David bent down to pick them up from where they'd landed near his tattered welcome mat.

In case his evening hadn't been sufficiently strange, David found a trio of other objects on the mat, placed at exact intervals. With the limited glow from his porch light, it took him a few seconds to realize what he was seeing. The thing on the left was a dead mouse, or possibly a vole, positioned with all its legs tight against the body so that it looked streamlined. The thing on the right was a similarly arranged dead bird; he assumed it was probably a young finch. In between, there was something shiny and metallic that looked like a small coin or a piece of foil, but he didn't feel like wiping rodent blood off its surface to find out more.

He'd received leavings like this growing up, when he lived in the Minneapolis suburbs and had outdoor cats who would return home with similar trophies. The practice hadn't gotten less unsettling.

David cleaned the mat using the broom and dustpan he kept near the back door, planning to bury the animals the next morning and assuming it was cold enough that there wasn't a rush to do so. He wasn't sure what cat left these tokens for him, though he had a pair of suspects. He finally collected his groceries and went inside, wiping his feet a few times on the mat's bristles.

His own pet, an orange cat with a pattern of cream-colored ribbons, greeted him at the door as always, headbutting David's legs as he removed his shoes and socks. "Hi buddy, I'm happy to see you too," he said as he put his bag on the kitchen counter and picked up Beauregard. "I know, it's been sooooo long. I haven't seen you in six whole hours." He usually made jokes like this about his cat's affectionate greetings, but he never tired of the animal's reliable excitement at his arrival.

Once the food was put away, the mail was sorted, and a restroom trip was completed, David flopped down on the worn armchair in his living room. He put his feet up on the ottoman and turned on the television, changing the channel a few times before he found Jimmy Stewart dressed in a football outfit and talking to a bush. Beauregard jumped up and wedged himself in the open space formed by David's outstretched legs and crossed ankles, staring at his owner and letting out a quiet meow. Knowing what the cat wanted, and knowing the neighbors both upstairs and downstairs were out of town and out of earshot, David took his tin whistle off the end table and played a few notes of "An Maidrin Rua." His pet joined in by meowing, one of the quirky behaviors David had discovered in his kitten nine years ago and used treats to reinforce until it became a repeatable trick.

A few seconds later, Beauregard was voicing a different meow and looking at something in the window behind the television. David couldn't quite see it, but his cat was staring intensely, with his body pointing in that direction like a hunting dog. David got up, turned off the television, and walked over, the orange cat running under his feet, and saw exactly what he had come to expect.

Another cat. This one sitting on the railing of the back staircase, staring directly into his home. Also black, also with a white spot, also bigger than an average cat.

"That does it," David said, to nobody in particular. He rushed into the kitchen, pulled on his shoes without bothering to tie them, and grabbed his coat from where he'd left it on the counter. He checked the door to make sure it wouldn't lock behind him, then sprang out onto the wooden stairs just in time to see the cat leap off the railing.

Before he could get a closer look, David noticed a strange texture under his foot and found someone had left a piece of paper on his welcome mat. When he bent down to get it, he could feel it was something thicker, some kind of strange parchment, and the stock showed a great deal of wear. The message on it, written in an elaborate script and with a fragrant ink, was something more familiar.

"Tell O'Toole that O'Flaherty is dead."

He also noticed that the dead animals and metal piece he'd earlier removed from his doormat had been moved, and found them on the windowsill near where the cat had been sitting, arranged exactly as they'd been when he first found them.

David walked over to where the cat had jumped down, and scanned the area below to see where it might have gone. The cat was nowhere to be seen. Instead, David saw a thin man pacing slowly in the alley. He wore a sweatshirt too light even for such a mild winter night, with the hood pulled up over his head.

"Hey you!" David yelled. "You, in the hood."

The figure turned, but with the sweatshirt hood over his head and with so little light in the alley, David couldn't see the man's face. The hooded man's head moved as if he was saying something, but he pointed at his own mouth, shaking his head to indicate he either couldn't or wouldn't talk.

"Did you leave me this?" David called down, holding up the piece of parchment and growing angry when the stranger nodded in response. "I don't know either of these people, and I don't know why everyone seems to think I do." He'd thought about it, too, searching his memory throughout the evening for any O'Toole he might have known in the past and recalling only a famous actor he'd never personally met and the name of a local bar that had closed years earlier. "Why do people keep telling me about this? What do they think I can do about it?"

Predictably, the man below him didn't answer, only nodding to indicate that he'd heard the complaints. David continued to list details about his night, about the repeated requests to convey the death of another person he'd never met, about the cats he kept seeing, about how he was just tired and wanted to go to sleep and be left alone to enjoy a needed day off from work. The hooded figure's body language made it seem like he was listening, but he said nothing in reply.

"You know what?" David said at last. "You want to tell O'Toole your news, why don't you find him and tell him yourself?" He was conscious that he was speaking a little loudly for two in the morning on Christmas Day, but there was no sign that anybody else in the area cared. The snow had truly started to fall by now, and David wanted to say his piece and then go back inside.

When David was done, the man in the hoodie raised his right arm and pointed at something on the other side of the alley, through the metal back gate of the vintage apartment building behind David's. He strained to see what the man was pointing at, trying to make it out through both the wind-blown flakes and the tightly designed links of the gate.

What David saw was the rounded shape of a small headstone, too far away for him to read the inscription. He could tell it wasn't made of familiar letters, but instead marked with some kind of symbols or runes. At first he thought this was intended as a threat, or a grim warning of the future, maybe a sign that O'Flaherty hadn't done what he was told. A second later, however, he could see something moving toward the stone. The black shape was difficult to see against the poorly lit sky, but it soon revealed itself as a cat.

Then David saw another.

...and another...

...until he soon realized he was looking at nine cats, all black, all the same breed as the three he'd seen earlier that night. For all he could tell, those three were among the ones he was seeing. The cats were moving in two rows, on both sides of a black, rectangular object that could only be a coffin. Eight of the animals were pushing it, with one cat leading the procession. The sight was strangely hypnotic, but soon the snowfall completely blocked David's view of the cats. When he looked around, he noticed that the man in the hoodie was also gone, his footsteps already masked by fresh snow.

Several times, David checked the spot where he'd seen the nine cats, but couldn't see them anymore. He couldn't even see the headstone, and began to wonder if he'd imagined the whole thing. After all, he was running on very little sleep, had been out drinking, and had experienced enough strange encounters in the past few hours that his imagination could be forgiven for getting away from him. He waited a few more minutes to see if he might be able to glimpse the funeral again, before the cold and his exhaustion urged him to give up and go back inside.

* * *

David's cat greeted him at the door, rubbing against his owner's legs, then sprinted away and planted himself next to his food dish, meowing. Figuring Beauregard was confused by his coming and going, David relented and gave his pet a rare extra meal, filling the bowl only halfway full of kibble. While the orange cat ate, David took off his coat, his jeans, and his long-sleeve shirt. Now dressed in the white tee and boxers that doubled as his standard pajamas, he took the piece of parchment he'd found on the welcome mat, balled it up, and shot it like a basketball into his kitchen trash can. He turned on his electric coffee pot and used it to boil water for a cup of herbal tea, which he spiked with a few drops of whiskey to help him wind down before bed.

With Beauregard at his heels, David took his hot toddy into the living room and turned on the television, where George Bailey was now being tossed out of a once-familiar watering hole. He took his fiddle down from its usual spot on his decorative but dormant fireplace and flopped down in his chair, while the cat took his usual spot on the ottoman. Figuring a song would help him forget the strangeness of his evening, David began to play "Carrickfergus" and sing along as best he could with a throat still constricted from the cold.

He was only on the second verse when his phone rang. At first, David worried some neighbor had canceled their overnight plans and his music was too loud for them. When he answered the call, he was relieved to find it was his grandmother in Killarney calling to wish him a happy holiday, repeating her pattern of miscalculating time zones ever since he'd left his home state. She apologized when he pointed out that it was past two in the morning, but he told her he was still awake and could talk. They went through their normal phone exchange, with David explaining that work was fine, that he wasn't seeing anyone but was working on it, that his parents were doing fine, that he was not in need of money but grateful for her offer.

When she asked what he was doing awake in the middle of the night, David was actually grateful to have someone to tell about his past few hours. He began his story with how he got home from work and went to the pub for dinner, explaining the cat and the stranger in the bar. He noticed that Beauregard seemed to take an interest in this part of the story, sitting upright and looking at him with the same concentration the cat usually reserved for requesting food or hearing his name called. David figured it must owe to his repeated use of the word "cat," one of the human terms he knew his pet recognized.

The cat continued to focus on David as he recounted the rest of the story. He told his grandmother about the homeless woman and how he gave her cat a can of food, and about the hooded man in the alley who left him a note, though he avoided mentioning the procession of cats, which he found too strange to share. "I almost forgot the most curious part," David said. "They all told me the same thing. They said that O'Flaherty was dead, and that I was supposed to tell O'Toole. I don't even know anybody named O'Toole."

While David's words prompted his grandmother to suggest possible sources of O'Tooles he could contact, they got a different response from Beauregard, one David wouldn't have believed if it had happened even eight hours earlier.

His cat spoke.

At first, it was in a language David didn't understand, something that sounded vaguely Celtic. It was definitely speech, not a meow or a growl, in a voice much deeper than the cat's normal pitch. The cat cocked his head at David, who had dropped his conversation and was staring in silence at his pet.

Beauregard regarded him for a moment, then spoke again, this time in perfect English. "O'Flaherty is truly dead?" the animal asked.

David just nodded slowly, too shocked to speak. "Then I am the king of the cats." With that, the cat leaned forward in a slight bow and then bolted.

David dropped the phone, though he could hear his grandmother's voice through the speaker, asking if he was still there. Before he could even get up from his chair, his cat had run into the old fireplace and up the shaft. David followed and looked up, but the animal had been too fast, and must have gotten out of the building. He ran into the kitchen, pulled on his shoes and coat, and searched the back staircase for the cat. He didn't see him anywhere.

Unsure what else to do, David spent the rest of the small hours wandering the few blocks around his house, calling for his cat and keeping an eye out for any more black cats with white spots who might provide clues. The snow was falling faster and the wind was getting strong, but he continued his search, checking every alley and driveway in the neighborhood.

David was still searching when the sunrise came, and the expanses of white around him reflected its early morning light. Not long after, the church bells nearby began to ring out for Christmas Day, and the quiet streets started to fill with people en route to their holiday plans. David took one more stroll around the area, wondering if he could explain what had happened to anyone else without seeming crazy.

Finding no clues and struggling to stay awake, David Silver felt he had no choice but to return to his apartment and wait for his unusual cat to return.

SEAWEED AND SALT

S he never had to wonder when the lady had been in the house. The trail of salt always told her.

Siobhan came in from the garden with two baskets of turnips. She had been digging up the tubers all day, brushing the silty seaside soil from each root with an old rag. The humidity gave her long, red hair the look of a distended bird's nest, and she wanted to draw a cold bath before preparing her evening meal.

She fumbled for the brass key in her dress pocket before seeing it was moot; the hillside cottage's heavy wooden door was already slightly open. Unsure who awaited her inside, Siobhan pushed her back against the door and slinked around its edge, trying not to make any noise. She found her dog busying himself with something on the floor, and, seeing that he was licking up some of the familiar crystals of dried salt, clapped to get his attention. The old corgi waddled over and instead licked the natural salts off the back of Siobhan's hand.

Siobhan called out to the lady, asking where she was, though she recognized she wouldn't get a response. Also, she already knew the answer. The greeting was more to alert the lady that Siobhan was coming, a case of prevailing manners.

The dog followed her up the ancient staircase, which creaked under each of her petite footfalls. The setting sun through the rounded window lit the stairwell, giving the stone walls a reddish tint. Siobhan considered taking a candle from one of the wall sconces, but reminded herself she wouldn't need it.

As she turned left off the stairs, she saw the double doors to the master chambers were open, and a thin bar of ethereal light filled the crack between them. The lady's flowing green dress always seemed to produce that light. Siobhan had never settled on whether the brightness came from the fabric, or whether the dress merely reflected the glow of heavenly bodies. The dog wedged himself through the doors, throwing them open, and Siobhan saw the familiar sight of the lady pacing the small widow's walk overlooking the sea.

She turned to look at Siobhan, and gave a polite nod of acknowledgement. The nod caused the dog to sit and wait attentively, while Siobhan used her hands to brush up as much salt as she could and wipe it off over the washing basin.

Courtesy made her feel like she should say something more. She could tell the lady she was welcome. She could ask her to please close the door next time so that the dog wouldn't run outside. Or she could thank the lady for the bucket of cockles and seaweed she always left in the kitchen as a kind of payment.

There was no point. Siobhan had said all those things before. The lady always acted as if she understood, though she never said anything in reply.

* * *

They met when Siobhan was still a young girl, when her grandparents owned the stone cottage. She had been asleep in her little bed in the corner until awoken by the strange luminescence. With a curiosity that surpassed her terrified ginger cat's, she had crawled out of bed and followed the light through the empty hall passage.

A few feet in front of her, she saw the lady's back as she cracked the door of the master chambers. Siobhan shrieked at the sight of the brightly lit stranger. The lady turned and approached her, and Siobhan scrambled backward into a corner of the hall, still crying with fear. Her grandparents didn't wake up, and the cat dared not venture out of Siobhan's room. She felt trapped.

"Leave me alone!" Siobhan yelled as the lady knelt in front of her. The visitor didn't speak at all, but put a finger to her mouth to urge the little girl to be quiet. She smiled as she did so, showing small dimples in her glowing cheeks.

Siobhan lowered her voice, her eyes still wet with saline tears, and examined the face inches from hers.

The lady's features were those of early middle age, with crow's feet forming around her eyes and few narrow lines etched in her forehead. Her long hair remained lush, in tightly spiraled curls, and she wore a thin diadem that kept it out of her face. Her dress sparkled with the same emerald hue as her eyes, which looked at the little girl with a mix of sympathy and curiosity. Siobhan thought the eyes looked kind, and they regarded her for a long time.

Once the little girl seemed calm, the lady picked up the basket of cockles she had dropped when Siobhan startled her. She gave Siobhan the collection of mollusks, still pungent with seawater and mixed in with dripping pieces of seaweed.

Siobhan took the basket and tried to touch the lady's sleeves, but the glowing figure moved just out of reach. The visitor pointed to the stairwell and used her fingers to mime walking, urging Siobhan to take the cockles down to the kitchen. The little girl nodded obediently and did what the lady suggested. She placed the basket in the kitchen basin, and dumped a bucket of well water over it to try dousing the salty smell. Then, as she began to scrub the dirty shells, she saw the lady's light through the barred kitchen window, moving away from shore.

When Siobhan awoke the next morning, she was curled up on the floor of her grandparents' kitchen, her ginger cat asleep against her. She told her grandmother what she had seen the night before.

"That was merely a dream," the old woman assured her, before sending Siobhan out to do her chores.

She protested that the basket of cockles had been a gift from the visitor, but her grandfather insisted they were dropped off by one of the villagers whose masonry he helped set, or whose sons he had taught the craft. Boiled for dinner, they tasted like any other fresh cockles Siobhan had ever sampled.

That night, Siobhan pretended to be asleep until she was certain from their snores that her grandparents had retired for the night. She searched the house, but the lady was no longer there. Only the salt that had brushed off her dress as it met the ground hinted that she was something tangible.

* * *

The second visit followed a few months later. It largely followed the same motions, with three key differences.

This time, the cat was no longer scared of the lady. He followed Siobhan out of bed when the light beckoned, and remained at her side throughout the stranger's visit.

Along with a fresh basket of seaweed-drenched cockles, the lady brought an additional gift. She handed Siobhan a narrow tin whistle. The girl had no idea how to play the shiny instrument; neither of her elderly guardians ever expressed any love for music. The lady spoke no more than she had last time, but showed with her hands how to put the whistle to the lips and how to use fingers to cover its holes in patterns.

The little girl tried it. The whistle gave a harsh squeak, and she worried it would wake her grandparents. It took a few more breaths before Siobhan could produce a clear tone. Her doing so made the lady smile and put her hands together in applause, though her palms coming together produced no sound.

Siobhan tried a few more notes on the whistle. The last one triggered one of her few memories of her father. She had none of her mother, who had not survived childbirth, as her grandparents gently explained more than once. Something about that note, however, recalled her father playing music to her in her cradle, before he was lost in a fishing voyage and his parents became Siobhan's only family. A tune she hadn't heard in years came to her mind, and she attempted in vain to play it while the lady looked at her kindly.

The third difference was less pleasant.

Siobhan returned to bed rather than go downstairs. She put the whistle under her pillow, and rubbed the cat until he fell asleep. She waited a short while before returning to the hall, assuming she could keep an eye on the lady. Her grandparents' door was open, and she followed the light inside. Both her elders remained in deep sleep, breathing in heavy rhythms. The room felt colder than usual, as the floor-length shutters that faced west were both flung open, and the lady had gone through them to the widow's walk.

In the chill air, the lady paced the little balcony. Her green dress shone as brightly as any of the stars as she swept back and forth, looking out to the sea. Siobhan watched, fascinated. She didn't know how long, but she watched the lady for a while.

As she stared, the lady climbed onto the top of the stone rail and launched herself out to sea.

Panicked, Siobhan lost all concern for secrecy and raced to the balcony, just in time to see the undulating water where the lady had silently landed. She was sure nobody could survive a fall the height of the hillside plus two floors of the cottage, but before her eyes the glowing lady's head emerged from the water. Seaweed mixed with her hair, she began to move out to sea.

The next day, Siobhan again told her grandmother what she had seen.

"How dare you!" the old woman had shot back. "Don't you ever lie to me like that. It isn't clever of you."

Siobhan insisted what she saw was real, but her grandmother slapped her across the face. She had never been yelled at before, and it was the first time anyone had ever struck her. Siobhan cried as her grandmother continued to scold her, until she was sent to bed without dinner. She didn't know what her grandparents dined on that night, but Siobhan found the cockles dumped in the yard, left to fertilize the turnips and parsnips.

They never talked about that exchange. For a few weeks, though, Siobhan noticed that her grandparents went to bed in shifts, like soldiers standing watch at a fort.

Siobhan never lied to her grandparents about the lady. She didn't tell them about future visits, and they never failed to sleep through the lady's flights from the widow's walk. Siobhan made sure to bring home cockles often enough that the lady's periodic gifts seemed unspectacular. Her one lie concerned where she got the tin whistle; she claimed she bought it from a peddler in the village.

The lady always requested that Siobhan play it, and always smiled as she listened to whatever tune she could conjure. By the lady's fifth visit, teenaged Siobhan had mastered the instrument.

* * *

Even well into her adult years, Siobhan could never determine the pattern behind the lady's appearances. Sometimes, she arrived in the heat of the summer, when briny dew covered the shoreline. Others, she braved flurries of icy rain to journey to the house. Several years went by between some visits, mere months between others. She arrived in dusk, in the darkness of midnight, or in the orange glow of early morning.

The only consistent thing was the lady herself. As Siobhan matured, she thought the lady looked a little older, but came to see that was only because the visitor no longer put on a happy face for a child's benefit. She always seemed tired in her permanent middle years.

As years went by, Siobhan lost her grandparents and her ginger cat to old age, though she gave each fine care until the end. She kept the hillside cottage, trading her garden's extra bounty for whatever goods she needed in the village. Years' worth of empty cockle shells formed a boundary around that garden, where she planted every summer and watched her corgi grow from a gaunt puppy into an overfed companion.

She kept her own bedroom, never moving into her grandparents' old space. It felt like it belonged to someone else.

* * *

The lady had gone more than two years since her last visit, and Siobhan always wondered where she went in between. Once she realized the source of her open front door was no local burglar or vandal, she let down her guard, reflecting that the lady who so scared her on the first visit had become a comforting presence.

With the lady's nod as a cue, Siobhan went back to her room for the tin whistle. It didn't shine like it once did, but its owner had mastered dozens of tunes. She played one for the silent lady, who nodded in thanks and gave another round of her soundless claps.

"You're welcome," Siobhan told her, and snapped her fingers for the corgi to follow her out of the master chambers. She long ago stopped watching the lady jump; she still found it unsettling.

Instead, she took a candle from her room and lit its wick off one from the stairwell, lighting her way to the kitchen. With the bucket of well water she'd brought in that morning, she began to wash her turnips along with the fresh batch of cockles, looking through the barred window as the glow appeared.

She watched it slowly wane as it moved past the visible horizon.

THE NEW SHEPHERD (A FABLE)

The fox had been hungry for six days.

He was not quite starving, but a fox could only live on corn kernels, summer squash, and grass for so long. He needed meat.

Someone at the Gregory farm had finally discovered the hole he'd dug under the chicken coop, with just enough room for a fox to wiggle inside and swipe a few eggs, or the occasional chicken. He found the perimeter newly encased in barbed wire, and he never had learned how to pick the lock on the main door.

"This," he thought, "requires a plan."

He used to get most of his meals from town, where humans threw away more than enough food to keep his tawny belly sated. Raccoons had closed that avenue for everyone by knocking over trash cans and spilling their contents. The fox understood people enough to know they would coexist only with those they didn't notice. "Ring-tailed fools," he muttered, reflecting on the troves of garbage the townspeople now kept inside at night.

Since then, he'd relied on the lone farm on the edge of town, a much longer trip from his den in the woods. The sun had come and gone dozens of times since then, and he'd done well for himself with the chickens. In that time, the farmer had taken the spring lambs to town, harvested his summer crops, and was now removing most of the corn from his fields.

Usually, the farm attracted its share of small rodents that could have tided the fox over, but an exterminator had been around. The fox cursed his effectiveness, and that of the scarecrows. Crow wasn't chicken, but it would do in a pinch.

"I could use a bit of mutton," he said to himself as he eyed the full sheep paddock. The challenge, of course, was the sheep all had a size advantage on him; even if he took one down, he'd struggle to get it through the fence. The border collie who guarded the sheep presented another problem. In these months of farm visits, the fox had always found the dog an attentive and intimidating presence.

After one more attempt to get to the chicken coop, the fox formed his plan. Once dusk fell and he confirmed the farmer was in for the night, he scampered to the wide paddock and hopped atop the surrounding fence.

As he expected, the dog rushed at him almost instantly, growling and barking. The fox quickly leapt to the highest fencepost, and flicked his tail just out of the jumping collie's reach. While the sheep pressed together, he counted more than four dozen full-grown ungulates, any one of whom could feed him for weeks.

First, he had to contend with the dog. "My dear fellow," he began, in the most charming voice he could manage. "I promise that I am as afraid as you wish me to be. I have no intention of killing any of your charges. I just want to talk to them."

"Then why don't you get out of here?" the dog growled. "You jump in this pen, and I'll rip you apart."

"Understood, understood." The fox placed his paws up in a show of surrender, though the dog still jumped and snapped at him. He raised his voice and called to the sheep, over the dog's barking, "As for you, I simply want a word. Call off your dog, and I promise to stay right here on this post."

"Why should we believe you?" asked one of the smaller ewes.

"None of you can fit through the fence, can you?" Their silence admitted agreement. "I couldn't drag one of you through if I tried, and even if I did jump in, the dog would make short work of me. Agreed?"

A few of the sheep nodded.

"Then please ask your canine friend to quiet down and move out of the way."

The fox could tell the sheep remained wary, but two went over and spoke to the border collie. The dog stopped barking, but still glared. The fox motioned with his paw a few times until the dog backed up, never breaking eye contact.

"Now, the rest of you, gather round. I have a business proposition for you."

"What could you have that we need?" asked the ram closest to the fence.

"Not what I have, but what I can offer. Your freedom from this farm."

"Why, so you can eat us?" another sheep answered.

"I am an honest fox," he said. "You're right that I could use a good meal of mutton, and that is what I hope to gain from our arrangement—"

"What did I tell you?" the dog yelled. "He's just another predator wanting to eat you. You're safe right where you are."

Here, the fox looked around him, making a show of checking that the farmer wasn't coming. "Safe? Where you are? You don't believe that, do you?"

"The dog keeps the wolves away, and the fence protects us," one sheep said.

"And who keeps you safe from the farmer?" The fox knew he had baited the hook properly. He decided not to mention that he'd never seen a wolf anywhere near the farm, or even in the woods.

The sheep talked over one another, and over the dog's attempts to butt in. "The farmer takes care of us." "Why do we need to be safe from the farmer?" "What are you talking about?"

"The farmer only takes care of you until it's time to eat you. All of you. Where do you think he took your spring lambs?"

"To the farm in town," several yelled back at once. That exchange quieted the dog, whose face fell.

"He took them to town, but not to any farm," the fox said, hanging his head. "All of them were slaughtered for meat."

Some of the sheep protested, but the dog's face was their confirmation.

"Wild predators like myself, we hunt the old and the sick, and kill only what we need to live. The monsters who keep you in this pen kill your children before they even have a chance at life. And what's worse, they don't even eat them all. If nobody consumes the corpse in time, they just throw it away without a thought, a complete waste of a life. You're afraid of me, but you allow this?"

The border collie had ceased staring at the fox, which allowed him to hop from the post onto the top slat of the fence as the sheep drew closer.

"Now, I admitted I want to eat one of you. But I'll only take one, where that farmer will eat all of you. Some of you soon, some of you after you give him another group of babies for him to kill. He would rather eat eight babies for the same meat I'd get from just one sheep. It's up to all of you to choose whether that happens from now on."

"Choose?"

"You can stay here and have this dog guard you until the farmer comes to kill you. Or I can let you out of this pen and take you to the woods. There's plenty of food, and far more room than you have here. I'll make sure no wolf comes, and all I ask is that after every twenty or so moons, you give me one of your number. You make your selection however you want, you take care of it, and just deliver the results to me."

Two rams cornered the border collie to keep him at bay while the other sheep conversed. The fox deliberately sat too far to eavesdrop, certain of the outcome.

Once the sheep agreed to his terms, the fox ran along the fence to the paddock door, and pushed the sliding lock until it sprang open. The flock streamed out the open door, save the two rams who kept the dog from following. When the rest were free, they exited and helped push the door back in place, so the fox could lock the dog in alone for the night.

Mimicking as best he could the dog's herding technique, the fox kept his word and brought all the sheep to the woods, arriving just as dawn was breaking in the east. "As you can see, you have all the space and food you need. I am going to repair to my den, but you will need to keep your end of our bargain before the sun sets again."

When the fox emerged from his den the next evening, he found a dead ewe the others had left a few yards away. He feasted for days, sleeping every night with a full belly and a relaxed mind.

As the seasons changed, the fox's plan continued to keep him well fed. He never asked the other sheep how they chose which of their number to bring him, or how they were killed. He never asked those questions as the sun came and went dozens of times, the next spring's lambs were left to grow into sheep, and the flock provided him fresh mutton from time to time. He never had to return to the Gregory farm or feel the need to risk his neck for the taste of chicken.

"Sometimes, I worry I've become a lazy fox," he thought to himself, "but I've never been anything but an honest one."

REDUNDANCY

Regina Maplewood had pored over dozens of files, for more hours than she cared to count. She had questions about several, but the one that most befuddled her was that of Charles Finnegan and Hartwin, the only pair of employees housed in the same folder.

Since her arrival from London, Ms. Maplewood had followed the same routine each morning. She would arrive before most of the staff, make a large instant coffee with the white powder meant to approximate cream, and take a brisk walk to the spartan records room at the far end of the building.

There, out of the employees' view, she spent the mornings becoming as familiar as she could with the whole operation. Budgets, personnel files, leases, expense reports — the endeavor made good use of her recent stint across the Channel in Grenoble. After her now-traditional lunch of a microwaved white-pepper vegetable pie and a fizzy lemonade, Ms. Maplewood filled her afternoons meeting with *Herald* employees, one on one or in small groups. She wasted little time on idle chat, and nobody questioned how seriously she took her work.

The *Herald* had long served this part of Northumberland as its primary local news outlet. While residents still read the larger papers to follow the goings-on in Parliament or with the national team, most remained subscribers as a way to keep up with what the local schools had planned, how the council estates were faring, and which denizens had earned which recognition from which charitable concern. Few businesses in the area had a wall without at least one pinned *Herald* story touting their accomplishments.

Nearly all the newspaper's employees were Northumberland born and bred, and Ms. Maplewood found their number to contain no shortage of the kind of local eccentrics her parents often associated with the north. Whether among the staff, on the streets, or in the town pub she frequented between ending her day's work and retiring to her tiny hotel room, people here seemed to carry a distrust of outsiders, and Ms. Maplewood surely felt one of those.

After all, she had come from the home office in London with the unenviable mandate to research and declare redundancies. As it had throughout its current streak of acquiring regional publications, the capital-based conglomerate that employed Ms. Maplewood liked redundancy suggestions to be made by recent graduates with no ties, sentimental or otherwise, that would stand in the way of reasoned, objective analysis. Thus did Regina Maplewood find herself on her first assignment, contemplating the value of everyone from the editors down to library archivists like Charles Finnegan.

Her interest in Hartwin, therefore, made obvious sense.

After all, who was more redundant than an imaginary friend?

* * *

Like many young boys and girls, Charles Finnegan spent much of his early life talking to a friend his parents could not see.

What made Charles unusual was that, now a middle-aged man and a respected professional archivist with an intuitive knack for organization, he continued to do so.

Nobody, not even Charles himself, could remember when he first met Hartwin. As an only child, Charles spent much of his time in his room, reading books and making up elaborate stories about what happened to the characters after the author ended their adventures. His working-class parents couldn't be described as neglectful; they had the means to ensure he never went without food or other necessities. Because Charles had always behaved well, however, the Finnegans saw no need for nannies or other forms of authority. When they were gone during the day, the boy entertained himself, and his parents spent most of their hours away from work at home with Charles.

The key phrase, of course, was "hours away from work." With so few of them, Charles had ample time alone to let his imagination roam free; at some point, it did so in the form of a boy his own age named Hartwin.

"He'll grow out of it," Mrs. Finnegan always said. She was incorrect.

While other children on the estate would convene an impromptu attempt at cricket in the alley or an elaborate game of tag in their front garden, Charles would kindly demur and prefer to spend time indoors with Hartwin. At family dinners, the empty chair at the four-seat kitchen table always needed to remain clear for the invisible boy. Mr. Finnegan often warned against "indulging the habit," but Charles remained precocious enough to carry on conversations with his parents in the supposed presence of Hartwin, and his social development seemed otherwise normal on all fronts.

Sure, it could be unsettling when the boy laughed at a joke Hartwin told or cautioned his friend that something was too dangerous, but Charles would usually relay what was allegedly said to his parents. As far as they could tell, Hartwin's humor was heavy on puns and alliteration, and his "dangerous" ideas mostly involved playing outdoors in inclement weather. He seemed harmless enough.

If anything, Hartwin was a good influence. When the Finnegans listened at their son's door, he was often telling his friend a story or even tutoring him. (Charles insisted that Hartwin struggled in literature and science, and that it was his responsibility to teach him so he didn't fall behind.)

Even at school, Charles always insisted that Hartwin sit next to him. In a classroom full of truants and aspiring taggers, teachers had more important battles, and allowed Charles to claim an empty chair for his unseen comrade. The boy's behavior and grades stayed exemplary, and at some point Hartwin became such a normal part of his routine that it seemed too late to say anything.

The same principle had generally applied in the nineteen years since Charles — and, by extension, Hartwin — had taken a work experience in the *Herald*'s research department, which led to a temporary placement, which led to their current roles as the library's two assistant archivists. At least on paper.

* * *

"I don't understand how this situation has been allowed to continue," Ms. Maplewood said.

She hadn't phrased it as a question, but Elaine Boyer took the silence that followed the young woman's inquiry as a sign to answer.

"It's a bit unusual, I'll admit," Elaine said. She chose her words carefully, knowing her job as head of research wasn't automatically essential, and that this afternoon meeting could be about her as well as her assistants. "Their work is excellent. They run the library, the archives. Any reporter needs to find out the snowfall on Boxing Day in 1949, or what we wrote about in someone's obituary from thirty years ago, they'll get the answer lickety split. Those two know our region better than anyone; I don't know where we'd be without Charles and Hartwin..."

"May I point out that you know very well how you'd fare without Hartwin," Ms. Maplewood said, crossing her legs and leaning forward. "Seeing as, best I can tell, there is no such person."

"You're right. Of course. Sometimes even I forget that. I'm so used to Charles talking to him. To tell you the truth, every so often I catch myself explaining something to Hartwin."

"But..."

"Oh, I know, but it's a good exercise for working out an idea aloud. Charles doesn't mind if I borrow him for a bit. It's like when I talk to my dogs. I know they're not going to answer me, but at least someone's listening."

"No, nobody's listening. That's my point. And yet, Hartwin collects a regular salary. Please explain this to me."

When Elaine took a chance on Charles all those years ago, she had expected only a few months of a poorly paid student helper. If that helper had his quirks, so be it; she was simply doing a favor for her widowed neighbor Mr. Finnegan. His health had prompted a premature retirement in Gibraltar, and he asked for help getting his unusual son a job of work.

She had expected the young man to be shy, or at least on the awkward side, but Charles was friendly and polite. He did give her an odd look when she hesitated before shaking Hartwin's hand (Mr. Finnegan had helpfully warned her in advance). Otherwise, he was an outgoing lad more than capable of talking football with the other young men in the break room, and several women rather fancied him at first meeting.

He didn't seem the type who preferred talking to an imaginary person, but every employee of the *Herald* discovered that tendency within a few days of his arrival. The newsroom tended to be a hub of gossip anyway, a side effect of bringing together dozens of people who always knew more than they could comfortably put in print, and the non-newsroom portions of the business were well-stocked with people excited by their proximity to such stories. The upshot was most anyone Charles met already knew about Hartwin and was good at disguising surprise when he would carry on what definitely seemed like one-way conversations. Plus, he benefited from the northern pride in decent manners. Everyone either treated Hartwin with respect, or did otherwise only behind his back. Hartwin had assured Charles he was fine with it either way.

Elaine had been as amazed as anyone at how indispensable Charles Finnegan and, by extension Hartwin, had become. At an office where most everyone took pains to work their precise hours, Charles preferred to come in midday and stay until late in the evening, happily updating the archives with the contents of that day's edition. It wasn't long before he'd memorized the filing system. Within just a few years, he had become so well versed in the region's back pages that he became the de facto repository of Northumberland history. Though, quite often, he would say he needed to consult with Hartwin when answering a query.

"That's all fascinating," Ms. Maplewood said after Elaine Boyer relayed the full story. Elaine's detection of irony lagged the younger woman's, and she didn't realize she was expected to add more. "But why are we paying a salary to an imagined individual? And how does he even cash his cheques?"

"Oh, that's not a worry," Elaine said, her round face beaming. "When I asked them to join the staff full time, I assumed we wouldn't be able to pay Hartwin properly, but Charles wouldn't stay without him. They talked it over, and agreed to split one salary in half between them. Charles takes it all on his account and gives Hartwin his share, seeing as they live together anyway."

"They didn't talk over anything. You're just paying Charles."

"Of course. I was just trying to answer your question..."

"This is all a delusion in his head, and all of you are enabling it. I can't understand how you don't see this."

"Maybe you should meet Hartwin and talk with him before you decide..."

By this point, Ms. Maplewood's slender fingers covered most of her face, and she looked at the floor when speaking.

"There. Is. No. Hartwin. Only a crazy assistant researcher." She looked up. "Let's say we were to make Hartwin redundant and keep Finnegan at his half of the pay. Do you think he would accept that?"

"Oh...I see," Elaine said. They were getting to the point now. "I don't know that Charles would be willing to work without him. They've been together so long."

"More likely, he doesn't think he can get by on half wages. He's probably correct, but we didn't create this situation at home office. More likely, we'll need to make both of them redundant, and you can replace them with a student on work experience. Someone who doesn't see people who aren't there. Maybe two, and they'll both exist."

"I think you should speak to Charles and Hartwin before you make any decisions. At least give them the same chance you've been giving to the others."

Word had spread around the office that Ms. Maplewood had been scheduling brief interviews with anyone she considered a potential redundancy. It wasn't entirely true — mostly she'd been trying to meet with leaders in every department, regardless of how secure their position seemed — but Ms. Maplewood was slightly curious as to what Charles Finnegan was like in person.

"Fine, I will meet with him after my lunch break tomorrow."

"Them, dear. You should meet with both." The younger woman started to reply, but Elaine cut her off. "I'll tell them for you; Hartwin can be hard to track down this time of day, and he doesn't always answer his telephone."

* * *

Ms. Maplewood had just finished her daily pie and returned to her files in the records room when, through the glass rectangle in the door, she saw a man waiting on the other side.

"Come in," she called out when he tapped gently. The door moved just a crack, and Ms. Maplewood beckoned the visitor in with a casual wave. "Come right in and take a seat."

The man who opened the door still looked like the photo in his personnel file, but it had to be a good ten years since that image was taken.

Charles Finnegan still had sandy brown hair like that in his picture, but its uneven shade indicated he'd been dyeing it for some time, and it had started to form a widow's peak. He had filled out some, with a football-sized paunch protruding under his shirt, and had a thin veneer of scruff over most of his face.

Based on his photo and reputation, Ms. Maplewood had imagined him some kind of clean-cut overgrown teenager, but Charles could have passed for any average man at any pub she'd ever visited. It only took a second for his more distinctive quality to shine through, however, as before entering he held the door open for a few seconds, then presumably followed Hartwin into the room.

She found the contrast more tragic than she'd anticipated.

"Good afternoon, Charles," she began, standing and leaning in for a handshake. "Please, take a seat."

"There's only one chair," he said.

"Yes, I suppose there is."

"Can Hartwin sit and I'll stand? He's been having troubles with his knees lately." Charles briefly looked offended, and directed his next comment to his side. "It's nothing to be embarrassed about; I told you to take your pills."

"Charles, I'd like to speak just with you. I apologize if that wasn't clear. Can Hartwin wait outside until we're finished?"

"That's okay with me, but you should ask him."

Ms. Maplewood nodded slowly and turned to her best approximation of Hartwin's position. "If it's alright with you, I'd like to speak with Mr. Finnegan alone for a bit. Thank you."

She knew it shouldn't have surprised her to watch Charles put one arm around empty air, turn his back to her and lower his head to whisper to his friend — though she was a bit impressed by how the backslap he gave Hartwin seemed to stop as if actually impeded by an object. He held the door open long enough for a person to exit before taking the seat across from Ms. Maplewood.

"Charles, did Elaine talk to you about why I'm here?"

"She said the company that bought us a few months back was going to take a look at our operation," he said, friendly enough in his manner. "Looking to see where the fat was on our end, and hoping to trim it a bit. I take it that's where you come in."

"Precisely. I'm trying to talk to as many workers in as many departments as I can while I'm here, and that includes the research department. I'd like you to tell me about your role here — how you started working at the *Herald*, what you do here, in whatever order you like."

"How I started? Well, at school, I'd always been an avid reader," he began. "My father used to joke that I wouldn't know if something happened on our estate that day unless the *Herald* wrote about it the next morning. When I was up for a work experience, I wanted to come here above anywhere else, and he asked Elaine if she might have something for me."

"Are your father and Mrs. Boyer close?"

"I wouldn't say close, but they get on. They were at school together, and both stayed around the area. Where are you from?"

"Me? All over, but I'm based in London..."

"Up here, people sort of hang around. Mrs. Boyer did a lot better than my father, but they saw each other in town, as you do. Run into each other at the pub, in the shops, you don't really lose touch. Anyway, she told him how I could apply. It wasn't nepotism or anything; we had to interview just like any other candidates, but Mrs. Boyer said we stood out and that we earned our keep permanently. We've been here ever since."

"By we, you mean yourself and your friend Hartwin?"

"We work best together. Buy one, get one, we like to say." He laughed as he said it. "Normally they just had the one spot, but Mrs. Boyer said the boss would let her make an exception."

Speaking at a fast clip, Charles Finnegan proceeded to explain the work he and Hartwin performed in nearly two decades with the research department. His account differed little from the tale told by his supervisor and his file, though he gave far more detail and tossed in a few clever anecdotes. Ms. Maplewood had expected him to be somewhat introverted, particularly without the crutch of his imaginary friend in the room, but found Charles perfectly personable and rather well spoken.

He seemed almost normal.

"I'd also like to ask you what Hartwin brings to the table."

"Why don't you just ask him?"

"We also like to get feedback on everyone from those who work with them most closely. Get a second opinion, you see."

"I don't know that I can be objective; he's my best mate, and we've lived together as long as I can remember."

"I understand. What would you say are his strengths, as they pertain to his role as a researcher and archivist?"

"He's a right genius," Charles said. "Anything he reads, he remembers. Hartwin's got a photographic memory. More often than not, he can tell me if the article was on the right-hand side of the page, or above a particular photograph. I can ask him if he remembered reading about, say, a cannabis arrest from 1973, and he'll point me to the right volume to find all the articles. I taught him how I reorganized the whole system; the archives were a bit of a mess when we started here."

Charles went on like that for some time, conveying Hartwin's importance to his work as roughly as valuable as his own eyes or hands, and brushing away any query about whether Charles could just as soon perform those tasks himself.

"If I'm being honest, if your sheet there says you have to choose between the two of us, I'd make me redundant and keep Hartwin."

"How would that work?"

"What do you mean? The same way any of your redundancies work, I would guess. Please don't misunderstand me; I'm happy here and want very much to stay. It's just that Hartwin needs the position more than I do. I have other work I could try my hand at; I've always fancied taking a year or two off to write a book of local history. For Hartwin, though, this work is his life. He'd be lost without it."

"I see," Ms. Maplewood replied, though this development struck her as spectacularly unforeseen. She thought her questions would have prompted Charles to defend his own position rather than that of his imperceptible companion.

"I would hope you'd see your way to giving him a raise. As you probably know from your papers, we agreed to split a salary seeing as we live together and share expenses, but we can hardly get by on only half."

"That's something to think about," she said, though she didn't plan to give the idea much thought. "I was also wondering, shouldn't there be a way to make these archives searchable on their own?"

"In the long term, of course, we could digitize all the material in the archives, and the system for locating it all, and let the journalists look up all the information themselves."

"I was a bit curious about that. Most of the larger newspapers have moved to that model."

"They must have more staff or more budget; that's a massive undertaking," he said. "Even with Hartwin, Mrs. Boyer, and myself working full shifts, it would take years to transfer everything, even without all our other responsibilities."

"Why hasn't that process started?"

"The people here prefer the face-to-face approach," Charles said. "They'd rather have someone like Hartwin find exactly what they need and someone like me explain it all than just type a bunch of words on a screen. On top of which, sometimes they don't really know what they're looking for until we find it."

Ms. Maplewood pondered his words, realizing she had much to consider as she stood and extended her hand. "Well, thank you for coming in, Charles." He thanked her as well, and she began rearranging her files for the next meeting.

When she looked up, she saw Charles Finnegan still waiting by the door.

"Don't you want to speak with Hartwin?" he asked.

"I'm sorry?"

"You said you were trying to speak with as many of the workers as possible, and he's waiting right outside."

"Fine. I don't see why not. Send him in."

* * *

And so Ms. Maplewood found herself seated across from a man who didn't exist.

Charles had held the door open for his friend, and told him he'd be waiting just outside. It was for his benefit that Ms. Maplewood greeted Hartwin and suggested that he take a seat. Offering him a cup of tea was a joke for her own benefit.

She sat in silence for a few moments, not sure what she was supposed to do with the empty chair, but still able to see Charles talking to coworkers on the other side of the door.

"Well, Hartwin, what should we talk about, eh?" she began, doodling absentmindedly on her notepad. "I've heard quite a lot about you these last two days. I expected you might be a bit more whimsical, maybe a talking animal or mythological being, but no, it seems you're just an imaginary thirty-something librarian. Bit disappointing, but hardly your fault."

Hours of talking to Elaine and Charles had nearly primed

her to expect a response. Realizing that only frustrated her further.

"So it seems your friend Charles is a perfectly fine employee. Diligent, personable, knowledgeable. The kind of person I'd be inclined to keep on if he didn't spend half his time talking to a colleague who isn't even there. And who, for some reason I've yet to determine, has convinced most of this office to play along with his delusion. Are they mad? Are they making sport of him when his back is turned? Are they just humoring him out of pity?

"What do you think? Hmm, interesting. No opinion, then."

Ms. Maplewood could see that the frustration of her visit to the north was finding its voice. For the first time since she arrived, she had an opportunity to vent without anyone there to judge her or question her performance.

It hadn't felt fair for the home office to make her first road assignment one that involved taking away people's livelihoods; she'd taken a job in the accounting department because she was good with numbers, not because she wanted to view human beings in those terms. She hadn't liked the way the *Herald* staff avoided her, viewing her as something between the grim reaper and a curious foreign object that found its way inside.

The most frustrating part, however — the part that felt like the universe playing one more cruel joke on young Regina Maplewood — was that the person to whom she finally vocalized all this wasn't real enough to pay attention.

"So, Hartwin, what do you think? Should I recommend making you redundant? Or Charles? Maybe Mrs. Boyer? Or all three of you? Maybe the *Herald* doesn't need a research department at all. Or maybe we bring in someone from home office who doesn't see imaginary people. Are you even a person? Maybe you're a rabbit, or a stoat, or a feral hedgehog. Who's to say?

"I don't even know anymore. Why don't you tell me what to do if you're so smart?"

Enough time had passed that she felt justified in ending the charade. She went back to her stack of personnel files, determining which employees she would still need to interview before her merciful train back to London the next evening.

The door opened a crack, and Charles Finnegan entered. "Why? What happened?" he asked quietly. She wasn't sure what he meant, until she saw him wrap his left arm around just enough air to contain a full-grown man, then exit while whispering something to the area he had corralled.

* * *

On her last day at the *Herald*, Ms. Maplewood's routine remained the same. She arrived early, prepared her passable coffee, and returned to the records room for a final perusal of files before preparing to make serious recommendations on the long trip back to the capital.

Given the outsized amount of her time and patience the paper's research team had exhausted, seeing Elaine Boyer already waiting outside the door hardly qualified as a shock — that came from the hardened expression on the woman's otherwise-cherubic face.

"Are you proud of yourself?" she began, before Ms. Maplewood had even hung up her coat. "I understand you have a job to do, but there's no reason to treat him so disrespectfully."

"I don't know what he told you," the younger woman replied, "but I showed Charles nothing but respect in my interview. In fact, I was rather more impressed by him than I expected—"

"Not Charles! Hartwin! The way you spoke to him."

"Excuse me?"

"He told Charles all about it. A feral hedgehog indeed!"

"I don't know what Mr. Finnegan thought be heard—"

"It doesn't matter. See for yourself." Before storming away in a huff, Elaine indicated the sheet of paper someone had slipped under the door of the records room.

The letter was brief, but direct. *I've tolerated enough ridicule in my day, but there is a line. Today, madam, you have more than crossed it, and I shall no longer provide my services to this concern. Charles is free to make up his own mind but, as for me, you can go right ahead and make me redundant. I suggest you do the same to yourself. Have an unpleasant day. Piss off. Hartwin.*

By the time the staff began to take lunch breaks, word of the letter had spread throughout the *Herald* office. Ms. Maplewood could tell as much from the muffled snickers and dirty looks various workers gave her as she purchased her pie and lemonade from their respective vending machines. Whatever fear her presence had created in those she was reviewing clearly traded places with ridicule.

Just going about her final rounds, she heard more than one variation on *The invisible man told her to piss off.* Even as she dragged her bags to the front of the office and waited for a cab to the train station, she heard passersby laughing.

The *Herald* office truly did have a penchant for gossip. She was not sorry to see it in her rearview.

* * *

Ms. Maplewood couldn't wait to leave the north behind and go back to her comfortable flat near Piccadilly, where she just blended in with the thousands of other young professionals. She spent most of the train trip, and her first few days back at her desk, preparing an extensive report on potential redundancies in the Northumberland office. She cited the resignation of Hartwin, and of an often-drunk warehouse worker who expected to get the axe from her, as early signs of increased efficiency brought about by her efforts. To her surprise, the rest of her recommendations were passed over, the bosses thanking her for her efforts but deciding against more redundancies in the short term.

As for Charles Finnegan, he did make up his own mind; he agreed to stay on at his original salary and half of Hartwin's, promising to remain just long enough to help Elaine Boyer with the huge undertaking of digitizing all the *Herald*'s records. He had been right that it would be a years-long project, what with having to scan, tag, and file every article from the newspaper's full history. The project lasted long enough that Elaine retired before it finished, she and her husband contenting themselves with their garden, evening soaps, and as much travel to seaside resorts as their pensions could comfortably handle.

By that point, Charles figured he might as well keep on until the task was finished. He never learned that Regina Maplewood's redundancy recommendations hadn't included him after all.

He hadn't talked to Hartwin since a few days after the resignation letter. Whether out of concern or simple curiosity, his colleagues had asked after him at first, but Charles told them that the two had a row over the sudden loss of income, and that Hartwin had left town.

Some of the *Herald* staff, of course, were just going along with the story, though plenty of people were concerned for Charles and brought him casseroles. Charles Finnegan had enough pride to say he "barely missed" Hartwin and "didn't think about him that often, to be honest."

It wasn't exactly a truthful sentiment at first, but it became more true as time passed. Until the invisible friend he'd lived with nearly his whole life became like any other mate from school or a cousin who lived abroad, someone remembered fondly but as a piece of the past.

At times, Charles wondered if he had even existed at all.

WHITE CLIFFS

E ven with his windows shut, Arthur could easily hear the rise and fall of the air-raid siren. Seconds later, his radio joined its chorus.

A couple of years ago, the dual tone was an almost constant presence, first alerting everyone to the German planes overhead and then providing the all-clear when London had held serve for another day. The looping sound always reminded Arthur of the stories he and his brother Davey used to tell while camping, when they would try to scare one another by moaning like ghosts or banshees on some far-off moor.

The sirens were scarier, of course. Still, Arthur months ago gave up responding to them. With the bullet still lodged near his spinal column and the field medic's admonishment against quick movements, he felt he was in more danger of falling down the stairs or being crushed by a crowd than of being bombed out of his flat.

Instead, he merely turned down the dial on his radio, which had been in the middle of *Sincerely Yours* with Vera Lynn

111

before the warning interrupted. Arthur liked listening to Vera. She reminded him of the girls he grew up with, and he appreciated that she didn't drop her accent like so many other singers. He could hear the East Ham railways in her voice.

Shortly after the sirens outside shifted their tone to indicate it was safe to come out, the one in his radio returned to sing of how there would always be an England. Arthur shifted the dial to the right.

"Turn that blasted thing down," a voice called through the wall. Two indelicate knocks followed.

Playing his radio loud always annoyed Thomas Dane, Arthur's grumpy neighbor in the next flat. Dane insisted that sentimental music had a deleterious effect on the boys at the front, softening their resolve. Arthur had started hearing that view more and more often, as if Vera's song wasn't right about their small island outpunching its weight. When France had fallen, with Russia under siege and starving, and the Americans content to delay until their own territory faced attack, England had endured.

"Sorry, can't hear you," Arthur replied with mock sincerity.

Dane's tune had been different during the worst of the blitz. Then it was Arthur wishing his neighbor would take a break from quoting the prime minister's radio speeches in a poor approximation of his public-school accent.

The way Arthur saw it, no matter how inspiring others found those speeches — and however much the prime minister's judgment had improved with age — he could never get completely past the Dardanelles. For the men of his family, fighting on the beaches usually ended poorly.

Arthur had been barely a toddler when his father, Edward, sailed to war. Davey hadn't been born yet, and would never know their father without a leg that ended just below the knee, the work of Turkish machine guns that turned the lower portion of it into mince. He'd trained six months in Egypt for a charge that felled him in six hours.

When Edward told his sons the story, he always said he was one of the lucky ones among the antipodean forces. Though he tried, he was too injured to run back into the gunfire that claimed so many of his friends; they died around him while he writhed on the sand. From that point forward, he'd refused to even attend Sunday roast dinners, saying the smell was too much of a reminder.

As Vera sang that England would always mean as much to the listener as to her, Arthur thought about fate. How if his father hadn't taken such a liking to Weymouth during his recovery, the boys would have grown up at the bottom of the world, safe from German bombers. Instead, Edward had moved them to London in the peace between the wars.

After a short intermission, Vera began her newest song, about the white cliffs of Dover. For all his years of practiced British stoicism, Arthur needed to run his handkerchief under his eyes whenever he heard the song. This time was no exception, despite more pounding on the wall from his neighbor.

Arthur had seen the cliffs when Davey came back from France two years ago, brought over on one of the small craft that had helped with the evacuation. The hardest Arthur could recall crying was at the sight of his younger brother, filthy and limping, smiling as he disembarked.

For weeks, all anyone seemed to talk about was the success of the evacuation, and of the ordinary heroes who put their own boats into the channel to bring back the boys. One of Arthur's neighbors even appeared in *The Daily Mail*, beaming alongside the rickety craft he'd captained.

Arthur, however, remained troubled by the images of his

countrymen lined up on the beach like Marmite soldiers preparing to be eaten by German airpower. News soon came, too, of the horrors endured by those left behind and captured. Davey's division had since redeployed, this time to northern Africa, to the very desert where their father had awaited action. Arthur liked to think his brother was listening to the same song on the radio, assuming he was still alive. Post took a long time, but he hadn't heard from Davey in weeks.

It didn't feel that long ago that Arthur had packed up his own troubles in his old kit bag and tried to stop the Nazi advance into Norway, returning with the bullet in his back as an omnipresent souvenir. He hadn't seen the white cliffs on his return trip, but the image still felt poignant. An image of home.

There was something else about the song, though, that got to him. The idylls of shepherds and valleys, the notion of a return to normalcy, still felt a far-off fantasy. The air-raid sirens made that hard to forget, after all.

The reality was that every day London survived felt like a pyrrhic victory. If the war ended tomorrow, all that effort would produce a country worse off than before it all started. And it wouldn't end tomorrow. Every day for years now had felt like fighting back a wave that kept coming stronger, and part of England washed away with each tide.

Much as Arthur hated the thought of proving Dane right about sentiment, he could taste the salt dripping down his face.

If the war ended tomorrow, he knew he would still have the precariously placed bullet. Davey's friends left behind would still be gone, and their father's leg would still be a memory. Thousands would never sleep in their own rooms again. And that outcome, a decimated shell of the England there had always been, was a far, far better thing than any alternative.

What made Arthur shed tears most, though, wasn't Vera's

voice, or the memory of Davey's return, or even all he'd lost in the bombings. It was the beauty of the song's promised, central image.

He had never seen a bluebird anywhere in England. As far as he knew, nobody ever had.

SENTENCED TO LIFE

I

"What do you mean I'm going to live?" In four decades of medical practice, Dr. Tomlinson had heard the full range of reactions to his news. Or so he thought. He'd seen stoic footballers bawl like children after news of a cancer diagnosis. He'd had captains of industry offer him large sums if only he could do something extra that would effectively overpower nature's will. He'd seen one unfortunate soul wet himself in excitement after learning that what seemed a case of a sexually transmitted infection was no more than a midlife case of the mumps. Dr. Tomlinson had presumed he'd presumably heard or seen every possible reaction.

This was a new one, this refrain of "What do you mean I'm going to live?" This was extraordinary.

The man seated on the cushioned chair across from the doctor didn't seem angry, exactly, or even sad. He seemed rather...annoyed. More than a bit irritated.

Martin McFadden was a small man. Certainly in his physical stature. He wore what looked like his father's hand-me-down tweed suit, and the glasses on his thin head looked comically oversized. He wasn't short exactly, but his thin frame, drawn face, and too-together shoulders helped give the impression of smallness. More to the point, Martin McFadden was thoroughly small in his station in the world. He'd worked nearly thirty-two years as a receiving clerk at a firm on Oxford Street, an exceedingly dull job he'd taken just days out of secondary, hardly searching before finding a small job that fit his small ambitions. For nearly thirty-two years, he'd made sure packages were all routed to their proper places, a model of undistinguished efficiency. He'd lived in a small flat above his regular that he'd purchased years earlier, in a marriage based on little but convenience. Few would aspire to Martin McFadden's life, but he'd always found it perfectly acceptable. Until the day he found a small lump on his fittingly small genitalia.

After days of testing, during which he'd been scanned, sampled, and studied far more than he cared to admit, McFadden was told that this small lump would prove his undoing. A gruesome, painful undoing that would take some two hundred days to be fully undone, give or take a rounding error. It was this very prediction of doom that Dr. Tomlinson had just recanted before this stunned man. McFadden, curiously, showed none of the exuberance of a man learning he would not, in fact, suffer a painful death roughly eleven days hence. The lump was still there, of course, but had been freshly diagnosed as little more than a decidedly non-lethal calcium deposit. Unsightly and unfortunate for sure, but cause for no great concern. What concerned Dr. Tomlinson at the moment was the singularity of his patient's response.

"What do you mean I'm going to live?"

* * *

What Dr. Tomlinson didn't realize, and what Martin McFadden intimately knew, was that this unassuming man had taken his diagnosis as seriously as he had the stringent rules of the Royal Mail. Martin McFadden, on the very day of his diagnosis, had gone home to his meager flat above the Galway Arms, pulled his leather-bound ledger from his bedside dresser, and started to meticulously mark down the rest of his life. Even calculating for the longest of his doctor's survival estimates, he'd determined his finances down to the exact quid, listed the experiences he'd failed to experience during his long career, and planned how much he could do in the time he had left. He hated the cliché, but he wanted to actually try living every day as if it might be his last. The problem with that philosophy, he now realized only too well, was that the day he'd thought would be the last of his life was now apparently just another random day in his life. Of which he'd apparently have many more. Many more he now lacked the means, the logistics and, quite frankly, the inclination to endure.

After always longing for a rich and fulfilling life, he'd spent the past few months actually living one. Now he had little more to live for, and he would indeed live.

II

Martin McFadden had exited his doctor's office slowly and obliviously, betraying no sense of the changes he'd made to his life between his diagnosis and its unexpected dismissal. He'd said precious little to the physician beyond that one essential question, mostly just nodding to confirm his understanding that his life would go on. Normally a man of consistent politeness, he left with a handshake but nary a verbal pleasantry, not even to the ginger secretary the newly liberated McFadden would have otherwise chosen to chat up.

On the way out, he put on his relatively new trilby, tilting it down so that it covered a bit of his prominent forehead. McFadden had never been the kind to own such a hat, an item that in his youth had seemed an ostentatious display of wealth. His father, displaying the pernicious carefulness with finances that the family surname too often suggested in the London of those days, had always made it quite clear to young Martin that such things were foolish and unnecessary. Without the need to plan for much longer, things once foolish and unnecessary had ceased to carry that stigma for the former clerk.

Still in something of a fugue state, he stumbled along, heading instinctively toward the temporary flat he'd contracted near Piccadilly and St. James. He took the steps down to the Tube as he had thousands of times during his life, keeping his hands stuffed deep in his trouser pockets by habit, to defend his money clip and wallet. He jostled his small frame through the mass of people heading home from their own small ambitions, minding the gap as he always had. Seated for most of his subterranean journey between a rather large woman who smelled simultaneously of korma and anise, and an unkempt elderly gentleman with a rather severe case of dandruff, Martin

McFadden finally gave himself the opportunity to reflect on his new reality and take stock of his position.

He'd come back to London to finish out his days among things and places familiar, and to have access to the care of the NHS. As a man used to dealing with timetables, he'd allowed that he might last past the eleven days remaining on the high end of Dr. Tomlinson's initial expectation, and had given himself an extra week's leeway in terms of finances and arrangements. Still, that small degree of prudence was all he had left to show for himself after the past few months of indulgence. He'd taken no photographs, as he had no inkling that he would have any need of them. He'd purchased no souvenirs for himself, and no gifts for any of the many people he assumed he was unlikely to see again. He'd made no plans, and precious few excuses. He'd left most of his worldly possessions behind in his — or more accurately, his wife's — flat, on the assumption they'd go unneeded.

McFadden had wanted to think the landlord at his temporary arrangement would unwittingly allow him enough time to vacate both the premises and the mortal world simultaneously, before the next installment came due. It wasn't any malicious desire to prevent the landlord from collecting his due; the man was a bit abrupt, but not a dishonest bloke. McFadden simply hadn't planned for this eventuality. He hadn't thought much before renting such an elaborate, well-appointed flat, given his circumstances; now he began to contemplate whether he could simply leave with his suitcase in the middle of the night, assuming he could even find another arrangement.

The Tube pulled into his stop, and Martin McFadden again jostled his small frame through a small throng of commuters. As he emerged aboveground, shielding his glasses from the midday sun's rays, he realized he had nowhere specific to go. He could go home, but it wasn't home in any real sense, just a posh converted hotel where his suitcase had lived for all of four days. He could go to his actual, bought-and-paid-for home, but suspected he'd not be exactly welcome there, at least not without concocting an appropriate excuse for his prolonged absence. Having no employment to go to would cease to be a relief in a little while, and he didn't think he could successfully sign on until he had a few other things sorted. He checked his pockets, and found he had about thirty quid on his person, enough to at least lubricate his thinking process, and set out to find a pub.

III

A pint of stout usually lasted Martin McFadden a solid hour or so; now it took him a mere twenty minutes to consume his second oatmeal varietal in the dark underground pub he'd selected at random. He had never been a teetotaler, but his meager allowances did allow only a quite sober approach to sobriety. In his recent travels, he'd sampled dozens of fermented beverages, from cordial to kumis, and built up a bit of a tolerance in the process.

"Another?" asked the jovial barkeep, and McFadden nodded solemnly, earning receipt of a third helping of the thick, brown brew. No sooner did he place his small lips on that of the glass than he felt a powerful pat on his right shoulder, and looked over to see Rob Beasley. A substantial Mancunian who clearly enjoyed his local chippy to an unhealthy degree, Beasley had worked at the same postal office as McFadden for the last three years.

A far less fastidious man, Beasley had long served as an irritant to McFadden, the kind who openly saw the post with the post as merely a means to an end, failing to take his work seriously. He also bordered on the boorish, which most often left the quiet McFadden tense and annoyed around him, glad that this subpar example of the bulldog breed occupied an office down the corridor, so that their interactions were limited.

There was no such space between them now, as the portly man had recognized him instantly and began to jabber at him with the kind of long, uninterrupted speech that inspired slow-burning rage in a man with limited northern exposure. Barely pausing for breath, Beasley informed his erstwhile coworker that the place was running as smoothly as ever, that Gillian in the adjoining office had gotten herself knocked up and now had rather spectacular breasts to show for her efforts, and that everyone in the branch was still talking about the day McFadden had taken his three decades' worth of pent-up frustration with the tedium of his employment out in one rather spectacular tirade and left the firm for good. The larger man obviously enjoyed himself, as he recounted the incident in great detail to the one who'd instigated it and therefore had the least need of a reminder, though he did embellish some of the key details in the way he would the story of a fishing expedition.

While the Manc prat prattled on, the former clerk sipped his stout in silence, ordering and finishing another as he merely nodded repeatedly in lieu of saying anything. Beasley did at one point break to ask what McFadden had been up to in the months since they'd last seen each other, but used it mainly as an excuse to describe his favorite aspects of McFadden's last day, from the obliterated supply display to the alerting of the smoke alarms to the look on the supervisor's normally unflappable face. Unusually for a conversation with Rob Beasley, or at least a one-way conversation with him, McFadden actually learned something from this interaction. Regrettably, it was that the idea of his returning to his old situation was clearly out of the question, and that his future revenue had to come from elsewhere.

Seemingly in a daze and with his ears ringing, the small man signed his credit card receipt, thinking for the first time about the months of card-based debt he'd accumulated without a previous worry about financing its elimination. He placed a few quid on the counter out of courtesy, assuming the barkeep deserved extra for having to endure Beasley's rapid-fire conversation for as long as it would take the ample man to drink his way to silence. McFadden managed a slight grin to his longtime antagonist and a firm handshake before extricating himself from the dim bar.

IV

The idea of signing on had never entered Martin McFadden's mind previous to this day, and yet he found himself in a long queue to do precisely that. His adamantly Tory father would never have approved, believing public assistance revealed a weakness of character and sense of entitlement more fitting across the pond. Then again, his adamantly Tory father had died prematurely from a coronary brought on by work stress and a fervent loathing of James Callaghan.

As he waited, McFadden found himself becoming self-conscious. His skin was still a bit tan from his overseas travels, which the bureaucrat administering his questioning would surely notice. He wondered if he had to have actively looked for a new situation before trying the dole. He pondered how to answer the inevitable questions about what kind of situation he sought, why he hadn't signed on after leaving his last post, and whether he'd been sacked or left of his own volition. He worried as to whether his never signing on before would make him more or less worthy of suspicion.

The one question from the frumpy woman at the desk that threw him off, however, was one he hadn't asked himself while he watched half a dozen people in front of him answer a few quick queries and seemingly get approved. She asked him for his address.

McFadden hadn't yet figured out how to remove himself from his temporary flat but knew that, absent some unexpected infusion of money, he wouldn't be able to afford to stay past when the landlord came round in two weeks. He did have the key to his former space above his regular, assuming Mrs. McFadden hadn't bothered to change the locks once he'd left with no explanation save a polite and long, but bloodless, note. His mum might be willing to let him stay with her for a spell.

Though he hadn't told her the real reason for his extended travels, wanting to avoid upsetting her until it was utterly necessary. On top of which, thanks to a generous gift from her son designed to save her the pain of watching his demise, she was on her own holiday with her church group in the Cotswolds for another two weeks, and therefore unreachable.

The office worker tapped her pen absently against her ledger and gave him a tired, frustrated look McFadden recognized from his own years of drudgery sitting behind a desk and tolerating the whims of the public. Worried his indecision might be wrongly taken as insincerity, McFadden just gave his temporary address, making a mental note to forward any post once he found a new arrangement. The woman's next series of queries — about why he had left his previous situation, what he had done in between, why he felt he was deserving of state assistance — produced the same inability to provide cogent answers. And his repeated delays in responding, as it turned out, did get taken as insincerity. Combined with the fact that his passport address did not match the one he'd provided, and his otherwise wise decision against listing his former employer as a reference, the interrogation ended with a denial of benefits, a cold stare from the woman, and the knowledge that, after months of planning the perfect short-term life, he now had no plan for a longer term.

V

Philippa Ferguson McFadden had never seen her husband in such a state as this in their twenty years of marriage. If calling him her husband was even accurate anymore.

She'd come back from the shops one afternoon in May after her daily excursion to procure supplies for the night's tea, to find no trace of Martin McFadden. She'd thought it unusual at the time, since like many men of his age, position, and disposition, McFadden didn't have any real mates anymore. On the rare occasions when he went down the pub, he usually did so alone, and mostly frequented the Irish hotel downstairs. He never had to work late, never engaged in any hobbies, never joined any social clubs, never followed sport closely, never seemed to have the initiative for a romantic rendezvous.

Most nights, their routine was rote. Philippa would prep the meal, usually some combination of beans or spaghetti on toast, fish fingers, and either potato cakes or chipped potatoes. Sometimes a pudding on Fridays or a Sunday roast, but otherwise standard fare. Her husband would usually arrive between half past six and seven, and the pair would take their tea on trays in front of the telly, Philippa alone on the three-piece suite and Martin on the rumpled recliner where he usually fell asleep at some point during the back half of *EastEnders*. For years prior to his mysterious disappearance, it was a rare event that McFadden even bothered to transfer his sated form from the chair to the bedroom.

There had never been any animosity in their marriage, as only strong emotions could evoke animosity or any of its parallel reactions. Which was why she was so surprised to find no explanation for McFadden's disappearance. Until, when she'd given up on his arrival that evening, helping herself to his share of the beans, watching an episode of *Casualty*, and retiring to bed, she found the note he'd left for her.

Her first concern was that her husband had decided to take the most drastic of measures, but the note revealed something worse in its way. Martin McFadden had explained everything in a few perfunctory paragraphs that painted his whole life to date as an overarching missed opportunity, outlined his solitary plans for what remained of his future, and gave a half-hearted apology for absconding with most of their finances and the previously unused matched luggage they'd received as a wedding gift.

The lone saving grace to McFadden's rather shoddy farewell was that the one thing of value he'd left his wife was a good story. The circumstances allowed Philippa to avoid a decline of her own circumstances, as they provided her with sympathy — from the dole office, from the firm holding her late father's annuity, from the landlady who gave her a few months' grace. And eventually, she was provided with sympathy, and more than a bit more, from the barrel-chested proprietor of the Galway Arms, who had seen one of his regular customers head off in a cab on the day in question without questioning it, but found he fancied his missus when she came by three days later in a quest for information.

Now her husband stood in the doorway of the modest flat they'd occupied at the same time for a long time, his skin and muscle tones looking healthier than they had in a long while, but his stooped shoulders and small frame looking utterly defeated.

In the time since he'd disappeared, Philippa Ferguson McFadden had many times put significant thought into the many things she could envision saying to her erstwhile partner on the off chance he ever showed his face again. As she slammed the door in that face, she decided she only needed to say two words.

"Bugger off."

VI

Once the visit to his former home had gone about as well as he had predicted, McFadden decided he had might as well enjoy a final pint at his old regular. He took his usual stool in his usual manner, and signaled the solidly built prop for a stout in the manner he usually did.

Roughly thirty seconds later, he exited with his shirt and trousers soaked in the drink he'd tried to order, and the sting of an unexplained and unexpected blow to his left cheek...

VII

Holding a value bag of frozen veg against his tender cheek, Martin McFadden absently made his way through a full canister of spotted dick pudding, picking out about half the currants with the edge of his spoon. The temporary arrangement McFadden had arranged for as a final resting place in London had been a good choice. The three-piece suite where he lay was remarkably comfortable, and in the past few days he'd taken to spending his evenings in that same spot, deep in reflective thought about the vast array of adventures he had managed to complete in what he'd thought was a limited timetable. That and the palpable dread of knowing his demise was impending but not knowing for sure what day it would impend or how painful the final few days would be. Those rather dark thoughts of previous nights now made him nostalgic in the face of greater uncertainty.

The lounge window looked out onto Piccadilly Circus, letting him watch the hundreds of people all fighting their way to the Tube at once, on their way home from their own daily drudgery. Having been part of such a mob each workday for so many years, he marveled at how it looked from above, how futile and pointless that kind of life now seemed to him, and yet how ineffectual he now felt without it.

This was the earliest time of day he'd gotten back to the posh flat since his return arrival in London, as he'd spent the few previous days on what he'd considered one last tourism binge. He had paid a visit to the Tate, made his annual pilgrimage to the Natural History Museum, toured Parliament for the first time, had an underwhelming time on the Millennium Wheel, seen a few musicals of varying quality in the West End. The kind of things a man his age in from Hull or Norwich on a short stay would have done out of either interest or a sense of obligation, but his very long stay in the city before this point had never provided him that urgency.

More tired in both body and mind than he was used to this early in an evening, he now sat deep in contemplation of a new and palpable fear, confronting the contradictions of his life to date that he'd long avoided. McFadden had never thought of himself as a man motivated by money. He'd said as much many times when his father had questioned his lack of interest in becoming a barrister, or even a proper banker. Watching the bustle of the Tube riders, he knew that had to have been an unconscious lie. There had been no other reason to take a situation like his. Now that he'd packed a lifetime of experiences into a few short months, he saw the nearly four hundred months of honest work preceding as a complete waste of time and effort for which he now had to show about seven hundred quid in cash, a quartet of nearly maxed credit cards he was incapable of settling, and a nice flat he'd have to leave under cover of darkness a few days hence. When McFadden's father would talk at the dinner table of a coworker who'd lost his savings on a faulty stock or an ex-mate taken in a pyramid scam, his mother had always said of those unfortunate men that at least they had their health, and for the first time McFadden felt himself unfortunate to have his.

He thought momentarily about the handgun he'd purchased as insurance in case the final round of pain proved too much for him, though he had serious doubts that even in that circumstance he'd be able to overcome his sense of self-preservation. Along with "Divorced, beheaded, died," it was about all he had left from growing up a confirmed Anglican. Hardly a believer at his age, Martin McFadden still found it prudent to avoid eternal damnation, regardless of how miniscule the odds. He considered using the weapon as a means of acquiring additional revenue, but knew he lacked the training to use it properly if the situation called for actual deployment. This was a terrible plan, but he did credit himself for at least contemplating active plans.

In the meantime, Martin McFadden still had a few hundred quid, and a place to sleep that was a considerable improvement upon his previous lot. After trading the thawed veg bag with a more substantial one from the fridge-freezer, he made a stop in the loo for the most inexpensive of all entertainment, and followed it with one of the most expensive, pouring a full glass of single-malt Scotch from the bottle he'd opened the night before.

VIII

When he woke from his whiskey-induced sleep, McFadden felt the need to get some fresh air, as the telly was showing the tail end of the evening soaps, and he felt a pending rerun of Richard Wilson's signature program would now seem more depressing than humorous given his unusual state of mind. McFadden had purchased a few stylish suits of clothes before embarking on his travels, correctly assuming he would command more respect from himself, women worldwide, and various hospitality staffs. He donned a sleek black suit, complete with a vest and bow tie, and went out for an evening constitutional.

Left to his own devices, he wandered aimlessly around the still-crowded public space of Piccadilly. He recalled an American transfer student at his primary who had eagerly anticipated a first visit to the Circus under false assumptions, and thereafter never quite warmed to the area. Or how his own father dismissed it for the term's other meaning, the elder man's staunchness offended by the bright lights and admittedly shameless advertising awkwardly bunged in among so many stalwart structures, in his eyes a sign of how London had lost its way after the character building of austerity. He used to joke that the Angel of Christian Charity looked like anything but, more like an archer unable to choose which insufficiently stiff upper lip to punish with its projectiles.

For most of his life, Martin McFadden had thought of Piccadilly as somehow unique in that garishness, but the past few months had taught him otherwise. A man who'd never left his small but distinguished isle had now seen Tokyo and New York, Dubai and Hong Kong, all of which were somehow both tackier in person and grander in scale than he had expected, and which made even this part of London seem closer to the

council estate where he and his family had lived before his
father's premature passing and his own premature marriage. In
his months abroad, he had seen a surprising number of sites
that surprised him by inspiring awe in him. Things like Stone-
henge and the Pyramids, the Barrier Reef and Kilimanjaro, all
of which he'd seen so often in images that he thought they
could be forgiven for proving underwhelming, but instead so
overwhelmed him that London at its busiest now seemed
inescapably mundane by comparison.

With naught to do but stretch his unexpectedly lively legs,
McFadden headed along Shaftesbury, choosing to see a film at
the old Saville. Martin McFadden had never had much time to
himself in his long career, with most days a series of transfers
from station to station, from home to the underground to
Oxford Street, back to the underground and back to Mrs.
McFadden and their glorified bedsit. What little solitary time
he'd had was often spent at the cinema, in this building that
once held the premieres of stage musicals and hosted some of
his generation's premier musicians on its stage, but which now
filled its historic shell with the same films one could watch
anywhere, including the competent but undistinguished spy
thriller McFadden selected to fill his evening.

IX

Two hours later, Martin McFadden sat in a simple chippy, enjoying a late-night cup of strong, American-style coffee with an attractive popcorn purveyor he'd picked up on the way out of the Saville, one advantage of the fading but still-present tan he'd acquired abroad that made him seem vaguely exotic in his particularly pasty homeland.

Before his erroneous diagnosis, McFadden had little skill in the arena of attracting such an attractive woman, but even a small and fastidious single man traveling with enough pocket money and a lack of concern for long-term plans developed a certain casual confidence that he hadn't yet unlearned. For the previous few decades, his interactions with strange women tended toward short pleasantries or small transactions like ordering a pie with gravy or a one-way bus fare. Thinking he was not long for this world allowed him the ease of approach and fearless attitude toward rejection he'd witnessed in the footballer or barrister types he'd been jealous of ever since around the third form, and that change had come in rather useful when he tired of solitude in his travels. He'd also found that he could be more honest when his transient thoughts of a given moment weren't going to be stored permanently and used against him for arguments well into the future.

His dinner companion said little that interested McFadden, though he knew that was largely his fault for failing to develop many interests. What she did provide him was a willing ear, the first he'd found in a day of largely silent stewing. At the risk of seeming depressed or deranged, he told the tale of his visit to the doctor, of his decision to live every day as if it were his last, and of his repeated attempts to make do with his newfound lack of finality. As he talked about his experiences since the diagnosis in detail to another person for the first time, he decided that the trade had been to his benefit in the aggregate, and that the life he'd spent the day trying to repair was not the one he should have been living. Even if he had limited options now, he wasn't without any. He could see if his mum would let him occupy his old room when she returned from the Cotswolds, and he could spend his free day tomorrow thumbing through the classifieds in the *Independent* in search of a hostel or boarding space he could occupy briefly until then, and could try to find a job of work he could fill for a short time.

He could always get himself sacked, and take whatever he managed to put aside with him on another international itinerary. The idea he found himself forming aloud was not to plan for a long life of quiet desperation, but to try to enjoy a more unmoored existence. He had now been to places where even a clerk's London salary could go rather far, places he could settle if he could simply put some small sums aside in the coming months. He didn't know if this plan would content him, or even if it was viable, but he knew the other options weren't.

The night, or rather the early hours of the next morning, did end with his new acquaintance telling him he was too depressing and exiting prematurely, and with Martin McFadden left alone at his table with the bill, the lingering smell of chip fat, and his thoughts. At the very least, though, McFadden had started to consider his circumstances, if far from ideal, at least something he could get through. A life that might not be too much a chore to continue living.

X

Dr. Tomlinson had experienced a similarly long day filled with worry, though his concerns mostly centered around having to explain to his superior how a longtime patient had been given such poor information, how a calcium deposit had masqueraded as a tumor, and how he would finish the large number of forms he had to submit to explain those anomalies. He'd spent a good chunk of the day, as well as an evening alone in his office with a takeaway curry, looking through Martin McFadden's file, studying his charts. The man's mostly benign family health history, fastidious routine of checkups, limited exposure to medications, and lack of risk factors.

The charts confirmed the formerly alleged tumor was nothing for the former clerk to concern himself with; that much was certain, no matter how many x-rays Dr. Tomlinson looked at or what other data he considered. What now concerned the doctor was a strange discoloration in the patient's lungs. It could hardly be the deadly pathogen the doctor suspected, one which had never appeared in England or elsewhere in Britain except in the bodies of veteran travelers who had failed to undergo the preventative regimen of recommended injections. He felt no need to give his superior another reason to question his judgment, not for something so singularly unlikely. Only a man traveling far from the proverbial beaten path and drinking untreated water would even be in the realm of risk, and only a man with no concern about his future would prioritize saving a few thousand quid above such a standard routine of prevention.

Knowing nothing of Martin McFadden's routine from the day he'd quietly accepted his diagnosis to the day he questioned its rescinding, Dr. Tomlinson saw no reason to worry the poor man. He'd been through enough.

SILVER AND GOLD

The letter arrived in a comically large envelope, larger than a standard manila one. Large enough that it could have held something much more important than a card-sized, handwritten note asking her to come to Los Angeles.

Carol Gold brought it home with the rest of her mail on her weekly trip to the box she maintained at the local post office. The handwriting on the return address looked familiar, but she didn't immediately recognize it. She didn't open it until she'd walked three miles home, placed her cane in its holder beside the back door, and eased herself into her overstuffed armchair. Her Social Security check had arrived, along with a postcard from her grandniece traveling in Morocco, her usual assortment of magazine subscriptions, and dozens of examples of the predatory junk mail aimed at less-savvy women of her age. Carol thumbed through the mail, sorting it into piles to recycle, to save for later, and to read now while watching her daily dose of televised game shows.

When she got to the large envelope, she saw it was sent from an unfamiliar place called Sherwood Pines. The letter it contained was written on stationery from the same facility, which identified it as a nursing home and hospice in Culver City, California. The penmanship was sloppy and uneven, obviously the work of a shaking hand. She only skimmed it at first, until she realized the name at the bottom was Dash Silver.

For a few seconds after reading that once-familiar signature, Carol Gold struggled to catch her breath. She hadn't seen or heard from Dash since 1951, though it would be inaccurate to say she didn't still think about him often.

She took her reading glasses from the glass end table and put them on, perusing the note three more times. It told her that Dash Silver, now ninety-two to her eighty-four, was dying of a chronic infection in his lungs, no doubt the result of his decades of chronic smoking. He said the doctors gave him anywhere from four to six weeks, which now meant three to five after accounting for the postal delay. He said his family was with him and the pain was manageable, but that he wanted to get all his affairs in order. "Part of that," he had written, "is I would like to see you one last time. I want to apologize to you for everything — in person if you'll give me the chance."

He had enclosed a voucher for a round-trip bus ticket from Berkeley to Culver City, good for six weeks, along with two hundred dollars in cash for a hotel. So the cost wouldn't be an issue. Carol was retired, so she had the time, and Sally Jarvis next door was used to taking care of her cat and collecting her newspapers any time she left town. She knew she could go; what she didn't know was whether she should. Whether she should dignify his request, and whether there was any kind of apology from Dash Silver she could actually accept.

* * *

"Silver and Gold," the industry papers used to call them. There had been a time in her early twenties when Carol used to collect such mentions in a scrapbook, carefully cutting them out of newspapers and magazines and slipping them into plastic sleeves to keep their yellowing to a minimum. Silver and Gold on the red carpet at an awards ceremony. Silver and Gold starring in *The Idol of Zanzibar*. Silver and Gold vacationing on the French Riviera. At the time, her old school friends usually found out what she was doing with her life via Dispatches of the World reels that occasionally highlighted the Hollywood exploits of Silver and Gold before the start of meatier Holly-wood offerings.

Never mind that neither was a real last name.

Carol Gold had been born Carol Goldschlitz, but had it legally changed at the suggestion of the talent scout who first discovered her performing a tap routine in what passed for a local theater troupe in downtown Berkeley. Her troupe, all young women who had attended the same Jewish day school and stayed in town, had booked a fill-in gig at the Hearst Greek, opening for the Reggie Walters Orchestra.

With the benefit of nearly seven decades' hindsight, she understood how random was the series of events that created her career. A Jewish girl her age and status was expected to marry young, have many children, keep a good home, and generally leave her decisions to others. Her career prospects existed only because of the crash, when the loss of her father's job and of his savings enabled him to see the value in having his daughters contribute a few dollars here and there.

Reggie Walters was the kind of entertainer most good-sized cities had, the kind who was always able to make a respectable living playing local venues, and booked the occasional night in Oakland or Sacramento, but wasn't quite good enough to rise to the next level. By definition, however, a big band was always discovering new musicians, and talent scouts were always trying to pick off the best ones and steer them toward better opportunities.

Carol didn't think of herself as one of the best even in her small dance group. She envied Judith's timing, the way she intuitively picked up any new step on the first try. She felt she could never hope to have Dorothy's athleticism, or Sandra's body, or even Ruthie's hair.

Unlike those girls, however, Carol Goldschlitz was funny. She danced well enough the night the talent scout noticed her, but what he really noticed was how she played to the crowd. The way her face could mug right along with the mood of every song without her feet missing a step, and the way she feigned ironic shock or bemused ennui during the underwhelming between-song comedy banter Reggie Walters performed. To the scout's mind, some of the other girls had more talent, but it was the same kind of talent possessed by hundreds of other girls their age who moved to Los Angeles every week. At least Carol Goldschlitz was different. After the show one night, he handed her a card and offered to get her a few auditions if she would commit to coming to Hollywood.

* * *

That decision seemed so easy back then. Rereading the letter in her hand as she sipped herbal tea, it seemed funny that she'd had no doubt about packing a suitcase and moving alone to a city she'd never before seen, but now had serious reservations about making the same journey to a city in which she'd spent the most memorable years of her life.

Then again, Carol Goldschlitz had never really been hurt. Carol Gold knew, better than most people, how quickly, and how permanently, that could change.

Carol spent the summer of 1942 learning that Los Angeles already had more than its share of women her age who were prettier, or less careful with their propriety, or even just luckier. Her first meeting with a studio executive didn't succeed, and neither did the next few. She didn't consider herself a religious type, but was just religious enough to be uncomfortable with some of the ways other girls her age earned their roles on screen.

She had been close to giving up the night she met Dash at a jazz club. Somewhere in the attic, she still had trunks full of memorabilia, evidence that their chance meeting had changed her life. As far as she knew, none of her current Berkeley neighbors had a clue that she had framed movie posters featuring her name and face, dresses and jewels she'd worn to award shows and premieres, photographs where she stood next to Gable and Garbo, Bacall and Brando. She'd thought more than once that Norma Desmond would have stared green eyed at her eventual posthumous estate sale. She was content to leave those mementos to collect dust, though she never brought herself to throwing them away. Sometimes she still thought the whole experience had been worth it, while other times she wished she'd wake up and still be a teenager.

* * *

Dash Silver wasn't quite a star when they met, but the studio had already decided he would become one. In person, he was handsome enough, but he was made for black-and-white film. On screen, his facial imperfections provided an ideal canvas, casting shadows in the right spots. Something as simple as a head tilt could turn him from a swashbuckling hero into a nefarious villain.

Their first meeting took place at an afterparty for *The*

Famous London Express, a high-society farce in which Dash had played a small, but memorable, role as a butler feeding information about the family business to the upstart rival whose sister he wanted to marry. The studio wanted to test him in a pivotal part, and early reaction to the film suggested he was ready for more.

Most of the party guests congregated around the leads, who posed for press photos and signed autographs amid the elaborate decor, while various local acts performed on a stage decorated like the inside of a luxurious passenger train. Having booked a spot as one of the chorus line dancers, Carol wore the same outfit as the other girls — a train conductor's hat and vest along with fishnets and heels.

Something other than the outfit must have stood out about her because, not long after the show portion of the evening, a soon-to-be movie star swooped in to light her cigarette. He introduced himself, and bowed to kiss her gloved hand. She gave him her best Mae West impression, with a little Betty Boop thrown in, and the two of them wound up bantering for what turned into a few hours. They found an unoccupied table in the midst of the more famous performers, and Dash made sure their waitress provided a steady supply of champagne.

Looking back on that night, Carol couldn't remember exactly what they'd talked about or what happened when. Whether that owed to the years in between or that night's alcohol consumption, she still remembered the feeling, the tingly excitement of meeting someone new and interesting. Of course, she remembered the tobacco taste of the kiss that ended the evening, and the aspiring star's promise to take her to dinner the following weekend. When she told her roommate about their encounter that night, Heather had said it sounded like the opening scene of a movie.

Others felt the same way that night. When the photographers had finished with their other quarry, they took a few stills of the young pair talking at close quarters. The studio executives noticed too, seeing an easy chemistry they thought the two good-looking actors could keep up on screen.

As agreed, Dash Silver knocked on the door of Carol's little garden apartment on the next Friday night and the two of them walked to the nearby theater. What she didn't expect were the bursts of flashbulbs when they arrived, or the excited reactions of the dozen or so photographers who rushed over and asked them to pose. Their first kiss had been noticed by only a few people, while their second would show up in *Variety* and on the society page of the *Times*.

It would be years before such attention was ever a surprise again.

* * *

After sleeping on the offer, Carol decided she would take the free trip. The Northern California summer had been colder than usual, and she thought the Los Angeles weather might better agree with her joints. She had nothing important on her schedule keeping her in town during the next few weeks. Enough time had passed since she left the southern part of the state that she didn't worry about showing her face there, and there were a few old friends she wouldn't mind looking up. She hadn't yet decided whether her dying former lover would be one of them.

Carol paid a late-morning visit to Sally next door. Along with returning a tea service she had borrowed the last time her nieces came for a visit, Carol made sure her neighbor would feed the cat once a day, take in her mail, and generally keep an eye on the place. While they talked over decaf coffee and sugarless cookies, Sally asked all the obvious questions about the trip:

"Where are you staying?"; "Who are you going to see?"; "How long will you be gone?" Carol didn't know all the answers but, more importantly, the barrage of questions made her uncomfortable. Rarely one to lie, she "realized" she had a phone appointment to keep, and went home. To be safe, she made her phone reservation for the bus ticket before she had even put her cane down, just in case Sally could hear her talking through the walls.

Two days later, she was no closer to knowing how long she'd stay or what she'd do while there. On the other hand, she had cashed in nearly expired reward points to book three nights at a hotel in Marina Del Rey. Though the cat tried his best to impede her progress, she packed a suitcase with five nights' worth of blouses and undergarments, along with two pairs of slacks and two pairs of shoes. The suitcase was heavier than she'd expected, but one of the younger women waiting with her at the corner helped her lift it onto the local bus, which took her to the depot in Emeryville. There, a porter loaded her bag, and she boarded the Greyhound that would take her eight hours south to her former home.

Six decades earlier, she never had to take a bus; Forum Pictures always sent a town car for its rising stars. For the sake of propriety, Silver and Gold may have arrived at parties in one car, but the studio made sure they were taken home separately. Because barely two weeks after they met, Maury Wallace had asked Dash Silver what he thought about turning his off-camera relationship into a celluloid one.

Maury had a way of making people think he was asking when he was telling. It made him a likable boss, without undermining his actual authority. It also made Carol a star.

Within days of that conversation, Carol Gold was signed to an exclusive deal with Forum. Her third date with her boyfriend was a dinner with the rest of the studio executives, and the seventh took place on a studio lot in Silverlake that was busy posing as a Parisian nightclub.

With the benefit of hindsight, it fit a dating pattern that blurred the line between what about their relationship was real and what was just part of a movie. The two dates right before the movie began principal photography were the first two nights Carol and Dash actually spent alone together. Even on those nights it sometimes felt like he was performing, whether with his on-the-spot quips or his approach in the bedroom, where she could tell he had far more of a track record than her nonexistent one. She liked the performance, though, particularly the way he said her name during sex. With his smooth drawl, which masked the son-of-a-sharecropper roots of Hollis Daschle Sellvere except in the case of certain vowels, Dash made "Carol" sound like an exotic moniker nobody else had ever been called. She found ways to make him say it as often as she could.

To most of the cast and crew, their first movie wasn't anything special, just another romance in an exotic location serving as a test balloon for the studio's newest discoveries. The crew had made dozens of these, most of them in and out of theaters in a few weeks. Nobody on set expected Silver and Gold to match the star power of Bogart and Bergman in what was basically just a second-rate knockoff of *Casablanca*. Dash Silver played an American spy in occupied Belgium, and Carol Gold was the sassy innkeeper who served as his liaison to the resistance.

Shooting days were longer than any work Carol had ever

done. And it was easy to lose track of time on a lot designed so that weather and sunlight weren't factors. Forum Pictures had a tendency to pay the minimum allowed under union rules, and to squeeze from its employees every minute to which the executives felt entitled. Needless to say, these tendencies didn't endear them to most of the crew, who spent many an evening loudly complaining about the situation over rye whiskey in the few local bars that attracted blue-collar industry types.

Maybe it was her upbringing, but Carol had more in common with most of the crew than most of the cast, so she and Dash would sometimes join for drinks at the end of the night. Other young starlets might have blanched at the dirtier jokes, but Carol already knew most of them and could tell them better. Dash would join, but never seemed as comfortable with that crowd, more likely to drink quietly while Carol made friends. Her lack of pretension endeared her to the cameramen and makeup artists, and it didn't hurt her career that she was considered enjoyable to work with.

None of that would have mattered if *The Antwerp Inn* had flopped, but it outperformed most of the studio's romances. The movie wasn't great, but it was good enough. Dash and Carol traveled with the film to a few major cities, and audiences were enthusiastic enough that Silver and Gold were officially a bankable property.

* * *

As she sat in traffic, with the bus stuck in a bottleneck on the 101 outside Salinas, Carol thought about everyone from those days and wondered if any of them were still around. She knew Dash's usual on-screen sidekick and former friend, the redheaded comedian, Harry Lucas, had retired to Vermont; he still sent her a card on her birthday every year. Maury

Wallace's death a few years earlier had made the paper. Most of the crew members had been older, so they were likely all gone.

In a few cases, she knew that for sure. Ron Sternshein, the portly character actor who led the union and used to invite Carol and Dash to his Sunday salon, had shot himself long ago. Gary Berkowitz, who made her costumes for a dozen movies, died of a stress-induced heart attack not long after he was outed. Carol had never known Debbie Downing's real name until learning that the woman who played her sister in *The Two Mrs. Thompsons* had died homeless and penniless just a few blocks from the bungalow where Carol and Dash had lived in Los Angeles.

She never watched the old pictures anymore. Sometimes when she stayed over at her younger sister's, they would watch the classic movie channel on cable, but Carol always requested that they flip if it showed any of her own work. Carol knew Judith still enjoyed showing her grandchildren what their elderly, but still striking, great aunt used to be. She suspected her sister thought Carol had a hard time watching herself on screen, or that she didn't like being reminded of the aging process, but it just made her think too much about everyone who wasn't around to see their own work anymore.

When the bus eventually passed the exit for the Hearst Castle, the young couple in front of Carol suddenly became animated, talking about how they would have to make time to visit it on their return trip. She listened to them talk about the real Xanadu, and its place in film history, and how that prompted them to start listing their favorite "old-school" movies. The girl included *The Carpathian Caper* on her list, calling it an obscure film, and Carol smiled.

That one had been her favorite, too.

* * *

Movie fans sometimes forgot that Silver and Gold lasted only three years as a couple onscreen. They made seven movies together, attended dozens of events, and appeared in more gossip columns than seemed possible. In real life, their coupling lasted just a few weeks short of three years.

For most of their relationship, it seemed Carol and Dash rarely had enough time alone to ever take stock of where things stood. The studio knew star power could fade at any point, and tried to reap the most it could from young actors before that happened. Between working, promoting, and romance, she realized the two of them rarely had time alone together with nothing to do. They knew each other's bodies much better than they did each other's thoughts, and their suitcases received far more use than their furniture.

When Carol received letters from her school friends, or bumped into them in person, some of them complained about spending too many quiet nights with their husbands, reading newspapers together or building jigsaw puzzles with the radio playing. What felt like a waste to them was a routine Carol found rather appealing, as she had begun to realize those couples knew each other in a way she and Dash couldn't quite match.

At one party in Tahoe, she met one of Dash's cousins, from a branch of the family she had never even heard about before. She didn't know he'd attended two years of college until seeing a donation letter from his alma mater in a stack of unopened mail. Dash liked to order for her in restaurants, but nineteen months in was still forgetting that Carol didn't eat shellfish and preferred black olives to green ones.

That lack of familiarity seemed more an annoyance than a real concern for Carol back then. There would always be time to catch up on those things once a few more movies were complete. Once their careers were established and they didn't have to work as often, they could slow down enough to have time for long talks and empty nights. In the meantime, she was having fun, and there was always something to do.

Carol had started to notice things with Dash felt different around the time they wrapped principal photography on *Avenue of the Americas*, an underwritten picture about a New York businessman who couldn't fight because of a bum leg, and the intrepid secretary who helped him supply the Soviets to take on the Axis. By that point, the OWI was paying studios to make the kinds of movies it wanted, and Maury Wallace predictably took the money.

Dash complained about being tired a lot during that shoot, and a few times suggested that Carol could stay out with the cast and crew while he went home to sleep, saying he could use the rest. She didn't think much of it at first; they were together so much that having a rare night to talk with other friends was nice, and she was more comfortable joking and telling old stories when she didn't feel like half of a team.

Even though she and Dash became famous at the same time, she'd always thought of him as the bigger star. He'd worked in film first, he was a few years older, and she enjoyed watching him act. Spending time with other actors, but without him, made Carol realize how often she defaulted to a supporting player in Dash's life. Interviewers usually talked to him first, and he tended to give boilerplate answers that Carol would enhance with a quip. Even the studio heads tended to suggest movies to Dash for the appearance of approval, while Carol was expected to go along with whatever they selected.

She hadn't minded taking that secondary role until the night when Dash's familiar drawl said a different name in bed. In that role, Carol refused to defer.

He swore it had just been a solitary mistake, but Carol began to see the pattern as soon as she started looking. Chandra was hardly a common name, and the only woman she knew who owned it was an even younger actress, one who played a voluptuous Russian temptress in the film and remained conspicuously absent when the cast got together.

Though she left their bungalow that night and stayed on Harry Lucas's couch, Carol couldn't avoid the subject with a man she saw every day on set. Dash was always a professional at work, and he apologized daily for what he had done. When Chandra stopped showing up, Carol learned it was because Dash had asked the director to find her a different movie, and the studio had instead let her go entirely.

Carol pitied her, but reluctantly gave Dash another chance, after a few weeks of apologies. He'd been the only real boyfriend she'd ever had, and she understood that her whole career was based on the idea of Silver and Gold as a package. Together, their names atop a poster meant people would come to the theater; separately, she had no idea what they meant. So she moved back in, and they went through the motions for a time. Their coworkers had almost universally taken Carol's side, so Dash didn't need to make excuses when he wanted to avoid camaraderie, and Carol often felt he was trying too hard to be charming when they were alone. Once filming was over, Dash casually informed her that he didn't feel the same way anymore, and that he had recently started seeing a dancing cigarette girl on the side.

This time, Carol wasn't surprised.

* * *

The bus was supposed to drop Carol a few blocks from the hotel, but the driver had noticed her cane and offered to let her off right in front. Though she could still get around easily, just slowly, she accepted the offer as a precautionary measure. It took her only a few minutes to check in and get settled. The room was small, but adequate for her needs, and she liked that her bags were carried by a bellhop in an old-fashioned uniform. If not for the size of the television and the fact she needed to leave a credit card number as insurance, the hotel felt like those where she used to stay.

She still had a few hours until the summer sun set, and had yet to decide whether she'd pay a visit to Sherwood Pines during her stay. Dash's enclosed extra cash had yet to be touched, and Carol felt no guilt about using the leftover money to visit a few once-familiar sights. The front desk called her a taxi, and she decided Hollywood and Highland would be her first stop.

The old movie house still looked the same as it did the year Silver and Gold attended the Academy Awards, just a few months before things fell apart. Carol didn't much enjoy Bob Hope at the time, but smiled when she found his handprints. She needed her reading glasses to identify most of the names in concrete, and determined quickly that what used to be a special honor had become disappointingly common. It made her hand-prints' absence somehow painful in a way it hadn't been before that moment. She remembered arriving there in a town car, wearing an emerald evening gown, and now her intended reflection time was constantly interrupted by performers in garish costumes, superheroes asking her for tips, and characters from movies she didn't recognize offering to pose for pictures. Tourists flocked to these aspiring actors, passing by a real movie star without even knowing her name.

* * *

If Carol had her way, she would never have dealt with Dash Silver after his second affair. Even after their relationship had ended, however, their contracts remained active. What became their last film together was supposed to be a whirlwind romance set in the Pacific theater but, though not for a lack of professionalism, they couldn't fake the spark they used to have.

The studio had made them keep their split a secret from the audience, so Silver and Gold attended showings and walked red carpets, but the movie's reception was unmistakable. The elements were all there, but the film was oddly joyless. Without their familiar screen chemistry, their last film together was their first and only bomb. Between its poor reception and the uncomfortable way its depictions of the enemy aged, Maury Wallace never even bothered to store the film's stock properly, letting it become the Silver and Gold film few people still alive had ever seen.

When Carol explained to the studio head what had happened with Dash, she found him surprisingly understanding. Still committed to getting his money's worth, Wallace cast the two of them in different films from that point forward. By the end of the decade, Dash Silver had developed some wrinkles, and his temples had gone white, but he remained a bankable property for the studio, playing detectives and pirates and Civil War generals. Carol Gold, however, became a purely supporting player as she aged, able to trade on her comedy skills and her name recognition in ever-smaller parts. There weren't many good roles for women who weren't attached to a male star, and Carol was made to feel old while she still considered herself a young woman.

She had made enough money to live a comfortably modest life. She rented a furnished room in a vintage hotel, and often appeared in stage productions, also sometimes working as a voice actress for radio advertisements aimed at housewives.

JEFF FLEISCHER

Gold without Silver wasn't a huge draw, but there were worse things to be in Hollywood than a working actress.

* * *

The morning after Dash revealed his infidelity, Carol had used a day off to head down Wilshire and finally see the tar pits her father had often talked about wanting to visit one day. Now she was back there for the first time since, regretting that she'd never had a chance to bring him to Los Angeles before he passed and that she hadn't thought to scatter his remains there instead of burying him in Home of Eternity.

She stood for a while, leaning against the railing over-looking the largest of the pits. Carol had left town before the pits added the models of Columbian mammoths bellowing as they struggled against the mire, but the tar itself was the same as it had been since the ice age, the occasional bubble appearing on the surface. The setting sun made the whole park look time-less, as if a major street wasn't just a short walk away, as if less time had passed since the last time the southern part of California felt comfortable.

She'd had a difficult time getting across the park's grounds without her cane and shoes getting stained from the little pockets of tar that popped up all over, but the view validated the journey. Not knowing quite why, Carol found something about that moment that helped her both decide to visit the hospice the next day and determine exactly what she would say to her dying former partner.

* * *

By the time Dash Silver reentered her life in the spring of 1951, Carol Gold thought she had fully moved on from him.

154

She'd felt understandably bitter for the first few years, as she found mostly supporting work while still seeing his smiling face on posters seemingly every time she went to the movies. After a while, though, she had learned to look back at their time together fondly. Even her diminished career wouldn't have been possible without it, and the good days had easily outnumbered the rest. She still drew crowds at parties with her stories, and the origins of some of her closest friendships dated back to that period. As she approached her thirties, she was mostly content with how life had gone.

That was true until the morning she walked out of her front door to get the paper, and was greeted by bright flashbulbs and five men in suits peppering her with questions about Dash Silver. They were talking fast enough that she couldn't pick up what had happened until she'd brought in the *Times* and unwittingly posed for several photos.

The bottom of the front page featured a picture of Dash in a suit waving to the cameras, like a reversed image of the scene Carol had just experienced, and next to it sat a smaller image of their famous kiss on a mountaintop in *The Carpathian Caper*. The accompanying article informed her that Dash was in Washington to testify before a House committee, as he had volunteered to identify former associates with supposed ties to the Russians. Mrs. Hopper's column suggested that the committee looking into Hollywood subversion found certain pro-Russian scenes from *Avenue of the Americas* particularly troubling, and was giving Dash a chance to clarify the record.

Carol had never been political, and realized she had never learned much of anything about Dash's politics. She did know that Ron Sternshein had been an outspoken union man and a thorn in the studio's side, and knew that men like him were being ostracized from the industry at an astonishing rate. Like a lot of people in town, she thought the matter had been settled three years earlier. She'd worried then about Ron and some of his Sunday salon regulars, and hadn't expected a new round of anxiety about her friends.

She phoned Ron immediately, and drove to his home in the Valley as soon as she felt certain nobody was lurking outside her place. Ron clearly knew Dash had his name in mind, as he was unshowered and kept smoking a fresh cigarette as soon as he finished the previous one. Carol tried to reassure him, as did the few other actor friends who came by with coffee cake and nervous smiles. The phone rang throughout the day, but Ron refused to answer it until he and his guests all crowded around the radio to hear Winchell's nightly report.

Dash had indeed fingered Ron, claiming that his union activities were evidence of sympathies with the Soviets, and more than a dozen of their mutual acquaintances. What Carol hadn't expected was to hear her own name. She'd never heard Dash use her legal surname, until Winchell played a snippet of him accusing Carol of frequenting Ron's salon with the other alleged Reds, saying she always chose to stay out late drinking with union agitators. His voice was calm and methodical as he described those nights of blowing off steam after long days on set as some kind of class subversion, pointing out how often everyone complained about management and wages.

In the months to come, Carol Gold would play Dash's words over and over in her head, though it was the quotes in Hopper's column the next day that she actually memorized; during the broadcast itself, she'd been too blindsided to think clearly.

She knew the accusations would bring trouble, but had no way of knowing just how thoroughly that day would change her life. She soon got used to seeing photos of her in Russian clothing from *Avenue* appear in gossip columns. When she went to the grocery store one afternoon, her landlord threw her possessions on the street and locked her out without notice. Many of her friends found reasons not to call or write anymore, and the limited work she had soon disappeared.

Her own subpoena was one of the last prompted by Dash's testimony, after several of her friends had gone to jail, fled the country, or ended their own lives. Though she dutifully traveled to Washington as ordered, she was determined not to follow Dash's lead. She refused to answer any question put to her by the committee, starting when the chair opened by asking her to state her name.

Most of the money she had saved during her career was spent paying the large fine to avoid jail when her refusal to cooperate earned her a sentence for contempt. Unable to rent or work any longer, she had no choice but to move back to her father's house in Berkeley and reclaim her childhood bedroom. The same one in which she still slept.

Through all that, she thought as she took a cab down Venice to Sherwood Pines, Dash Silver never apologized to her.

After nearly three decades, he did make some public comments repudiating his testimony, saying the committee had threatened his livelihood if he didn't cooperate. That earned him forgiveness in some circles, usually from younger people who'd only seen Silver and Gold films on television or on video. Many shared her view that Dash didn't speak up until the country's politics had changed and there was no risk in doing so. Still, enough people who couldn't know what Carol Gold had dealt with began to treat Dash like a victim rather than an accuser. Those types, along with others who simply wanted to put the blacklist era behind them, even honored Dash during an awards show. Carol couldn't bear to watch, though she was glad to learn about half the crowd had refused to stand or clap for him.

When they arrived, Carol asked the taxi driver if he would wait for her, assuming it would be hard to find a return cab. Sherwood Pines was an immaculate marble building, erasing any questions Carol had about Dash's finances. The front door required some kind of pass to open, so Carol used her cane to ring the bell for the receptionist.

The nurse who answered and introduced herself as Angela was not much older than Carol had been when she met Dash, and looked like she could have arrived in town with her own plausible dreams of stardom. When the nurse asked how she could help, Carol explained that Dash Silver had asked her to come down for a visit. The younger woman looked confused and began to flip through a chart of names before Carol realized she needed to ask for Hollis Sellvere. The kind of smile that clarification prompted told Carol that even a dying Dash must have retained some of his charisma.

Carol tried to hand the nurse a sealed envelope containing the note she had written the night before on hotel stationery. Instead of taking it, Angela explained that while Dash was in his final days, he was awake and alert enough to talk, and insisted that Carol deliver the note personally. Carol hadn't felt nervous on the drive over, but that changed as she was led down the hallway to Dash's room.

The nurse left her at Dash's door and said to go in whenever she was ready, telling Carol to stop by reception if she needed anything else. Once she was alone, Carol took a few breaths and thought about how she could best supplement her note.

She looked through the thin glass opening on the door, trying to get a glimpse of Dash before he saw her. Though only part of the room was visible, she could see he was propped up on a wide bed, with a bag of fluids in one arm and an electronic monitor against the back wall. He was difficult to see because hospital blankets covered most of his body, and Carol could only make out a wrinkled hand covered with liver spots.

As she leaned forward to get a better look, the top of her cane knocked lightly on the door, and Carol heard a whispered croak tell her to come in. She was about to do so when she heard the voice again, but it was repeatedly saying Angela's name and asking her to enter. Instead, Carol took the envelope with the name "Dash" written on the outside, slipped it under the door, and walked back toward reception.

When the nurse asked why she was back so quickly, Carol simply explained that everything she needed to say was already in the note. She smiled, thanked Angela for her time, and returned to the waiting cab.

Part of her had wanted to write a long treatise, explaining all the effects Dash's betrayal had on her, and another part wanted to detail how she'd put her life back together in Berkeley and gloat about how full life was now while he lay dying. Had she entered the room, she knew she would have landed on one of those options.

Instead, she'd settled on a simpler solution the night before. One sentence atop the piece of stationery read, "What you did should never be forgiven," followed by a two-column list of every name he'd provided to the committee. Sternshein and Berkowitz, Downing and Lucas, and all the others she could remember.

They filled almost the whole sheet of paper, with just enough space left for Carol Gold to sign her own name.

PAYING THE PIPER

When the phone rang early Thursday afternoon, the Piper didn't answer it right away.

It rang a few times, the dusty receiver vibrating on its base, before he realized what was making the noise. Honestly, it had been so long since anyone called the landline that he forgot he even had it. The landlord had set it up years ago, and, since it wasn't a separate bill, he never thought to disconnect it. The Piper eventually rolled himself off the edge of his bed and ambled to the desk.

"Yeah," he said, but heard only a dial tone in response. He hung up.

He looked at the clock. It was already half past two. If he had to be awake, the Piper decided he'd might as well make something for breakfast. No sooner had he undone the twist tie on a loaf of bread than the phone rang again.

"Please hold for the mayor," a woman's voice said before he could offer a greeting.

"You called me..." he began, before the hold music clarified that nobody was listening.

His curiosity piqued, he held the receiver and listened to a lyricless version of a blues standard he hadn't heard in sixty years. He tried recalling the name of it. One pitfall of having a perfect ear for music was every melody he heard implanted itself somewhere in his brain. Occupational hazard. As for living forever, one pitfall was he couldn't always remember all the details, and sometimes spent far too much time on them.

"Is this the Piper?" a man's voice broke through the music.

"What does it matter—"

"This is the mayor. I need to talk with you about an opportunity. You can serve your city—"

"Let me stop you right there. I don't do that anymore. Not for a long time."

"I believe we can make it worth your while. Just take the meeting."

The Piper looked around what he still called his home and office, though it was more accurate to just call it home. He hadn't had time to make up the sheets on the bed before taking the call, but he hadn't done so in years anyway. The peeling wallpaper could use an update. He'd really fallen behind on dusting, too; that was probably worth fixing before agreeing to let a government official come over.

"Fine," he said, "though I can't promise anything. When do you want to meet?"

"Now. Downstairs. The car's been waiting for you."

The Piper went to the window and peered through the dusty metal blinds, adding cleaning those to his mental chore list. The light hurt his eyes.

The car that had pulled up wasn't the limousine he was expecting, but a sleek black sport-utility vehicle, the kind he didn't see often in the city. A large man in a navy suit and sunglasses stood next to it, his arms crossed over his chest.

"I'll need a few moments to get dressed."

"Whatever you're wearing is fine—"

"I'm wearing nothing. You woke me up." It wasn't strictly true, but a torn and flimsy pair of briefs was hardly appropriate for the occasion.

"It's two in the afternoon—"

"Give me five minutes. I'll be right down."

After hanging up the phone, the Piper went to the bathroom mirror and took a quick view of himself. From the deep bags under his eyes to the uneven salt-and-pepper stubble it always took him at least two weeks to grow, he looked rougher than usual. He didn't have time for a shave, but splashed some water on his face. A quick sniff of his armpits made him lather up a washcloth and spray a bit too much deodorant.

He briefly considered whether to throw on the pied outfit hanging in his closet, but he hadn't worn his trademark suit since before the war in Hamelin. Back then, he'd seen soldiers use colorful clothes as an excuse to arrest suspected gypsies, and had changed his style to better avoid notice. Since coming to America and giving up his old vocation, he'd kept it around as a reminder of his old life, but hadn't even tried it on in a decade.

Instead, he pulled on a baggy blue sweatshirt and a pair of black jeans with the knees worn out. He combed his unwashed hair back and threw on a felt cap. The phone rang again while he was pulling on his work boots, but he knew it could only be the mayor's office urging him on, and opted to run down the stairs instead of answering.

He was already regretting picking it up the first time.

* * *

"You the Piper?" asked the large man, whose bulk was more impressive up close, suggesting he served as some kind of bodyguard.

The Piper nodded, and tipped his cap.

"Funny. In that getup, you look more like the world's oldest hipster."

"And you look like an ape the mayor sprung from the zoo. Guess he keeps you around for your brains."

The big man opened the door to the vehicle, and slammed it hard after the Piper was inside.

Up front sat a young woman in a business suit, who must have been the caller, while the muscle slid into the driver seat and hit a button that noisily raised a partition.

The mayor sat facing the front of the vehicle, and motioned with his hand for the Piper to take a seat directly across. The Piper recognized him immediately; he looked pretty much like he did in newspaper photos, except lean enough to suggest cameras really did add a few pounds. Despite his short grey hair, he looked young for his age, and his large eyes gave him a somewhat predatory look. He sat with his legs spread and his hands in front of him, touching his fingertips together in a thoughtful-looking pyramid.

Once the Piper sat, the mayor leaned forward. Just enough to look the shorter man in the eye, without invading too much of his personal space.

"I am sorry for the short notice, but there's a matter I need to discuss."

"How did you find me? That's an unlisted number."

"It's my business to know everything that happens in this city. But I don't think that's your real question. You're wondering how I knew you even existed."

The Piper nodded in acknowledgement. No need to say more until he knew what was happening.

"A few years ago, I heard about a man living in a converted office downtown and that if he walked down an alley whistling, a few rats would follow him. The first time I heard about it, it felt like a rumor, but worth remembering. By the third time, it was something I had to confirm for myself. Three's a trend, after all. Once I saw it, it didn't take me long to put things together."

Even though he tried not to do anything musical outside his place for that exact reason, the Piper knew he'd sometimes gotten sloppy. Having an ear for music meant songs stuck in his head easily, and it took a conscious effort not to hum or whistle. The longer he'd hidden, and the better he got at adapting to his surroundings, the less attention he tended to pay. Seven centuries on the run did that. He wasn't aware of any rats following him lately, but there was no reason to doubt it.

"I filed that information away for the day I needed it," the mayor continued, "and we seem to have reached that point."

"If you're planning to turn me in—"

"Turn you in? No, no, you misunderstand me." The mayor leaned back and laughed, before returning his fingers to their pyramid shape. "I need your help. I have an election coming up in six days, and I want to win."

"We all want a lot of things. What does that have to do with me?" The Piper didn't follow local politics closely. Still, he read the paper often enough to know the mayor was leading in all the polls, but was in an increasingly tight race against a younger and better-funded opponent. A poll last week called the race a statistical dead heat.

"I've been looking for a problem I can solve quickly. Dramatically. Something the average voter's going to notice.

"Something like eliminating our city's rat problem."

There it was.

"That's a big job. It's going to cost you, and it'll need to be in cash."

The mayor rapped his knuckles twice on the roof of the car. The partition across from him opened, and the female staffer passed back a thick leather briefcase. It was heavy enough that the mayor needed a second effort to lift it to his lap. He then swung it around and opened it so the Piper could see the stacks of hundreds inside.

Even though the Piper hadn't yet worked out a price in his head, the suitcase contained more than he could have imagined requesting.

"One of these once you agree to the job," the mayor said, closing the briefcase and patting the top. "And another when it's done."

"Consider your rat problem solved—" The Piper reached for the briefcase, but the mayor pulled it back. He leaned forward so far that the two men's noses were almost touching.

"Not so fast, my friend. There are a few rules I need you to follow. Get it done by Sunday night, so people come out to vote Tuesday with it fresh in their minds. Do as much as you can at night if you don't want everyone knowing who was behind it. And don't even think about screwing me on this."

The Piper nodded and took the money. "And if you know who I am and what I've done, I'm sure I don't have to tell you what happens if you fail to pay me."

"It seems we have an understanding."

"One question. What do you want me to do with the rats?"

"The way I heard it, you drowned them in the river last time. Just like you did all the kids. We have a perfectly good river."

"You heard wrong on all counts. I didn't kill anyone, man or mouse, or any variety of either. Merely sent them away."

"Then how —"

"Trade secret. Can't give that one away even for all this money. Keep your side of the bargain, and it won't matter anyway. Now, I think our work here is done?"

The mayor nodded, and the Piper slid toward the door, wedging his rear end out of the soft seat and trying to minimize the noise it made. He saluted once he exited the vehicle, but the mayor held the door for a moment before letting it close.

"Remember, Mr. Piper. It needs to be done by Sunday night."

* * *

Once he brought the briefcase upstairs and hid it under his mattress, the Piper took a long walk in the autumn evening, putting together a plan.

That the city's rat problem had gotten out of control hardly qualified as news. Every time he walked down an alley, the Piper found blue or black dumpsters teeming with enough garbage to keep even the most discerning of rodents fat and happy. When dusk shifted to night, a careful observer would see rats ducking between fences or hugging the sides of buildings as they tried to get the first seating at that evening's feast.

Even the exterior wall of the vintage brick office building where he lived had a stark yellow sign showing an angular drawing of a black rat either screaming in pain or growling in aggression — it could be taken either way — and a red line crossing it out. Lots of buildings throughout the city had the same signs; others had ones with a more accurately rendered, fuzzy rat and a more subdued color palette. Either way, the signs detailed the city's current plan to eradicate the rodents. The point was to warn people not to feed the rats, and to be aware of the poison the city left out for them, in case a curious dog wanted to investigate.

Poison was never something the Piper liked. He found it needlessly cruel. And, based on his new assignment, it must not have been particularly effective.

The Piper stopped near the river. He leaned over one of the safety rails and let the murky smell of the water fill his nostrils. As he gazed out at the glistening skyscrapers and heard the honking and commotion of traffic, he started to understand the scale of his assignment. If he was going to earn his payday, he had much to do.

* * *

The next morning, he set to work. He'd kept his old pipes in their case for decades, hidden between the mattress and frame of his Murphy bed so they would be the first thing to grab if he ever needed to flee in the middle of the night.

The outside of the case had accumulated a thin layer of dust, and he had to wipe it down with a spare shirt, but the pipes inside were spotless despite the time gone by. "G usually works well for rats," he said aloud as he chose which of his instruments to play. Like a master sniper, he assembled the long pipe, twisting each piece into place. The old cork inside was still smooth, and the pieces fit easily. The thin reed had cracked, but he had a dozen spares banded together inside the case. It would take a few tunes to soften the new one, but he needed to practice anyway.

"Okay, here goes." He put the pipe to his lips. The first few notes were squeaky, and he cringed briefly, glad this particular pipe played at a frequency too high for his neighbors to hear. At least the human ones. A few more attempts, and the notes started to sound right. After a few scales to warm up, he practiced a tune.

He played one he'd used to draw rats before, something

he'd first heard from a Saxon troubadour long before the plague. He wondered if it would translate. Were rats on this side of the ocean susceptible to the same music? And did their reactions change with time? The Piper worked his way toward the window as he played, trying to catch a glimpse of any rodents affected by his song.

Then he heard them.

The walls started to shake slightly, as if feeling the after-shocks of an earthquake. More telling was the noise of pounding feet along the building's wooden bones, growing louder as they moved higher. He stopped playing when the sound felt too close, as the flimsy drywall near the door started to bulge from the weight of the stymied rodents in the walls.

"Don't know my own strength sometimes," he said as he began disassembling the pipe and packing it back in the case. There was no reason to wait until Saturday; the rust he had feared wasn't an issue.

There was plenty of time to nap before sundown, and still wake up early enough to really practice his breathing. It was going to be a long night. But two things were clear. First, and most importantly, he could still play.

Second, it might be a good idea to find a better apartment once he got paid.

* * *

"Do you see that?" Rhonda Tilson asked. She'd had a few drinks, but nothing unusual for a Friday night. Certainly not enough to conjure up what she glimpsed coming from the alley a few doors down from the bar.

"I didn't see anything," her date answered before resuming kissing her neck.

"Seriously, what is that?" She'd started work at six that

morning, and the bar had just closed at two, but exhaustion didn't make her hallucinate. "Look, over there."

The clouds blocking much of the moon's light obscured some of the motion against the darkness, but she knew what she was seeing. Rats were running out of the alley. Rhonda had seen plenty of rats around the dumpsters near her northside apartment. What she hadn't seen was so many rats moving in unison. At first, it was just a few of them, loping like small greyhounds. Soon, though, came a swarm as wide as the alley, rows of rats running in formation.

"What the...ew," her date said as he turned to see the street around them flooding with rodents. "Let's get in the car." He looked queasy.

As they turned and speed-walked to where the sedan was parked, Rhonda thought she saw a man out of the corner of her eye, walking alongside the rats. It looked like he was playing an instrument, though Rhonda couldn't hear any music.

* * *

By the time the Piper stumbled up the rickety steps of his building's wooden back entrance just before midnight on Sunday, and collapsed from exhaustion in his favorite chair, the city was nearly free of rats.

Not entirely. There were plenty of pet rats in cages or otherwise kept inside, but nobody was going to be upset about that. There had to be some older rats with hearing so poor they couldn't hear his songs, but they were few in number and not likely to reproduce. The Piper found it unfair that he wasn't able to get lab rats out of their predicaments, but the music only drew them; it couldn't get them through physical barriers.

His breathing was labored, since he'd spent the late hours of three consecutive nights walking around the city. As out of shape as he was, that would have been a challenge even without playing music the whole time. His lips were badly chapped from the reed and mouthpiece, and a few of his fingers had cramped from working muscles he'd allowed to atrophy.

A sense of satisfaction came over him, and he felt he'd earned the chance to fall asleep in the armchair, listening to some music on the old transistor he kept on the end table.

In his dream, an unexpected alarm broke his concentration while he was performing an important task; the details disappeared as soon as he woke up and realized the noise was actually the ringing of his landline.

"For the love..." he rose from his seat with some difficulty and got to the phone. "Hello?"

"Please hold for the mayor," the familiar voice said.

"Ugh."

When the mayor came on the line, the Piper couldn't help telling him, "You know, you can just call me directly without the whole hold routine."

"Sure," the mayor said with a slight laugh that indicated he'd never do so. "Come downstairs. I want to talk to you."

Another peek through the less-dusty blinds confirmed the black car waiting outside.

"Keep your pants on, and give me a chance to put mine on..." he began before realizing the mayor had hung up.

The Piper changed clothes without putting down the receiver, pulling off the sweaty shirt that clung to his torso and dropping the pants that were heavy with accumulated perspiration. He changed into baggy shorts and an old Aloha shirt, which felt both overly casual for a mayoral meeting and appropriate to his level of concern about that.

Minutes later, he was again seated across from the mayor in the back seat.

"This morning I took a long jog," the mayor told him. "The

same route I always take, an hour before sunrise so there's almost nobody else on the path. Do you know what I noticed?"

"That sleeping in sounds like a better idea?"

"That there were no rats. Usually they're out eating at that time, before the city really wakes up. It seems you did your job well."

"You know what they say. Any job worth doing. Now, about my money."

The mayor smirked and brought out a second briefcase. The Piper couldn't help but skim through the stacks of hundreds to make sure it was the right amount, but his benefactor didn't say anything.

"It's been a pleasure doing business with you," the Piper said as he closed the case and started to edge out of the car.

"One question first."

"Sure."

"Where did you put them all? The rats?"

"Nowhere anyone can find them. I assure you, it will be like they just walked into a seam in time and never came out." The Piper said it in a matter-of-fact tone, as his explanation was the actual fact.

"You killed them, right? Are they all dead?"

"Of course not. I'm not a killer. They're just existing somewhere far away, where they don't need to bother anyone. They'll age and die like any other rat, but no faster or slower."

"Is that what you did with the children? In Hamelin?"

The Piper said nothing, but he slammed the door hard behind him.

* * *

The local news called the election Tuesday night just ten minutes after voting closed.

171

The present and future mayor had clearly expected the Piper to hold up his end of the bargain. Since Monday morning, local television and radio hardly let a commercial break go by without at least one campaign-approved ad about how the mayor had "cleaned up" the city's rat problem and how he had plans to bring the same can-do attitude to other major issues. "He's just getting started," in the parlance of the new slogan.

Watching an ad at a bar on Monday night, the Piper was struck by the clever merging imagery that made clearing the city of rats suggest a bigger effort to clean up corruption and inefficiency. Left unsaid was why the cleanup had waited until days before the election. The Piper's role also didn't merit a mention.

Still, a race that had shown the mayor only slightly ahead for the last few weeks turned into a landslide.

The Piper hadn't voted; he'd never even registered, part of his plan to stay as far from the grid as modern reality allowed. He didn't have a strong opinion either. The mayor had solved his financial situation for some time, and he understood why people saw it as getting things done, but any deal done with briefcases of money struck the Piper as betraying a certain lack of transparency. But, the young opponent seemed like an empty suit elevated only by being the other option compared to a generally unpopular mayor.

Besides, the Piper had quite a lot of cash on hand now. He spent Election Day fixing up his unit, and bought a burner cell phone so he could unplug the old receiver from the landline.

* * *

The next few months passed without much excitement. The Piper's routine returned to normal, though he allowed himself a few more indulgences. Without fear of attracting rats from the alley, he took to practicing his pipe a few nights a week, playing in the keys he used for the rodents but careful to avoid any tune that might risk recalling them from their current location. His playing had been strong when he did his work for the mayor, and it reminded him how much he enjoyed making music.

Nearly a year after the election, he was in the middle of assembling one of his pipes when he heard a loud pounding on the door. Not expecting a visitor, he waited before answering.

"Piper, we know you're in there. Open up."

He couldn't place the voice at first, but recognized the mayor's massive bodyguard once he looked through the peephole. He unlatched the door.

"What are you doing here?"

"We called you several times. You didn't answer."

"I got rid of the phone. Nobody calls that number but your boss's office."

"And it didn't occur to you that we might call you again? Never mind. Come with me. He's waiting in the car. It's an urgent matter."

The urgency was clear on the mayor's face. Already a thin man, he looked gaunt, with his skin tight on his face and the lines around his eyes more pronounced. He motioned for the Piper to sit, and the partition was already up.

"I'll get right to the point," he said. "If you've watched the news lately, you know I'm in kind of a tight spot."

The Piper hadn't watched the news, but he'd read the free weekly paper. A bribery scandal wasn't a new problem in this city, and he couldn't say he was surprised, considering the two heavy briefcases wedged under his mattress.

"I'm not sure what that has to do with me. The city's rat problem is still solved as far as I know."

The mayor crossed his legs, and made a pyramid with his thin fingers.

"Last time we spoke, you told me you were no killer, but you didn't answer my question about the children."

The Piper nodded, but said nothing.

"Is the story true, that you rid the town of its children as easily as you had of its rats?"

"If you know that story, then you know that mayor refused to pay me for my work. There's no reason for you to worry about the children of this city. Unless you're planning to ask for the money back."

"No, no. You misunderstand me." He paused before continuing, choosing his words carefully. "If the story is true, then you can draw humans to follow you the same way you do rats."

"Sure. If I have a reason to."

"And you don't kill them. You merely send them somewhere like, how did you put it? A seam in time?"

"Theoretically."

"And if you wanted to, you could call them back?"

"If I remember how to play one of the songs that does that. What's your point?"

The mayor grinned. "So there's really no harm if you were to, say, clear certain people out of the city. At least for a while..."

The Piper had pieced together part of where the mayor was going, but he still wasn't sure of the details. "So you're not even going to pretend you're innocent?"

"It's just money. You understand."

"If you think people won't notice your accusers suddenly disappearing, I know some detective movies you should watch."

"I know that, and that's not what I was going to ask. I just need another initiative. Something bold to get the public back on my side. Like they were after the rats went away."

The Piper said nothing, but motioned with his hands for the point to hurry along.

"As you know, our city's had a homeless problem for years—"

"No."

"Just for a little while. You can bring them back when this blows over."

"Not interested."

"I'll make it worth your while. There's more where those other briefcases came from. Shall we say double the fee?"

"Which part of *no* don't you get?"

The mayor's expression changed. "Maybe people would be interested to find out you're real, alive, and living among them. We can play things that way if you'd prefer."

The Piper just glared at him and shifted out of his seat.

"But a whole town's children are fair game?" the mayor called out before the car door slammed.

* * *

The mayor must have been confident that the Piper would take the job, because an ad aired during the next day's morning news touting the success of his plan to solve homelessness. The office had tried to cancel what had been an expensive ad buy, but one instance on one station didn't get deleted. For a few days, the ad boasting about a homeless solution that didn't exist became the most talked-about story in town, even more than the mayor's financial misdealings.

Three times that week, the bodyguard knocked at the Piper's door. First, the large man asked for another meeting. Then offered another bribe. And, finally, a direct threat. "Take the homeless job, or the mayor goes public saying that it was your plan, and that you asked for bribes to carry it out."

"Nobody's going to believe that," the Piper said from the other side of the door.

"They know the rats are gone. Once they know who did that, they'll believe it. It's not like you haven't done it before." The henchman slipped a phone number under the door. "You have two days."

The Piper watched through the blinds for the vehicle to pull away and, as soon as the coast looked clear, slipped out the back stairwell and flagged down a cab.

Knowing the mayor's office was desperate and wouldn't stop bugging him, the Piper decided to stay at a motel on the west side of town for a few days. He brought his pipes, his briefcases of money, and a suitcase with a few changes of clothes. Just in case, he switched cabs in a parking lot on the way, though he didn't see anyone following him.

Late that night, in his quiet hotel room, the Piper practiced another song he hadn't played in centuries. He stayed up long past his usual bedtime, since he only had two days to get it right.

* * *

"How can I help you?" the mayor answered his phone. He didn't recognize the number on the other end, and almost nobody had his direct line.

"Please hold for the Piper," the Piper said in a sing-song voice, whistling a few notes before talking into the phone.

"Cute. Have you reconsidered my offer?"

"I think we should talk. Thought I'd come to you this time."

"When? I have a window this afternoon—"

"Oh, I'm in the hallway outside. This shouldn't take long."

The mayor opened his office door to find the Piper sitting in one of the waiting area chairs in his faded Aloha shirt. The Piper smiled and put his pipe to his lips. The mayor couldn't hear the tune at all, but in a few seconds heard a rumbling.

He screamed as the stampede of rats came pouring through the hall and headed directly toward him. There were too many to count as they chased him back into his office, and their combined weight prevented him from closing the door. The mayor kept screaming, though the layers of rats crawling over him muffled the sound.

The Piper continued until no more rats arrived, by which point the office doorway was mostly obscured by moving piles of fur. He quickly disassembled the pipe and put the pieces in his pockets as he exited the building. On the way out, he tossed his burner phone in the trash.

It felt like a good time to find a new town.

SPARE CHANGE

When Robertson awoke, he was rather surprised to find himself standing on a curious shore.

The last thing he'd remembered was crossing the road in front of his apartment, popping down to get his morning paper and coffee, a routine he'd followed nearly every weekday for eight years. He no longer even bothered to change out of his flannel pajamas, as this way he could finish his morning brew and read the sports section even before his shower and subsequent commute.

Feeling his slightly greasy and disheveled hair, Robertson realized he hadn't gotten around to showering that morning. And, for the life of him, he couldn't remember who'd won last night's game. He was still wearing his plaid pajamas and warm slippers as he scanned the dark water in front of him.

The surface seemed entirely free of movement, as still as his tub before an evening soak. Not even a ripple appeared as the small wooden boat came toward him. He could see that a lone man propelled the craft, urging it forward with one elongated oar that repeatedly penetrated the river without disturbing its stillness in the least.

The man wasn't familiar, not exactly. It was more that Robertson felt his presence was expected, like a postman or a meter reader. He was clearly old, but of some indeterminate age. His white beard, stooped back and tightly pulled skin could place him anywhere from his late seventies to the highest end of human endurance.

The boatman docked the rickety craft on the shore where Robertson stood, somehow keeping it steadily in place without any kind of anchor. Now using the oar as a cane, he propelled himself forward in the same way he'd propelled his boat, shuffling onto the land with the long, jerky steps of a man too long at sea.

"Good morning, sir," he said with a bit of a lilt in his deep voice, and gave a toothy smile. "Just the fare, please, and we'll be on our way."

Robertson realized he had only the vaguest notion that he should be on that boat but, when in Rome...

He set about rummaging through his pockets, only to find them empty. He wondered if he had forgotten his wallet when he went to get the paper. Instinctively, he ran through all the secondary checks of the absent-minded commuter, but nothing in his chest pocket, his pants, or his slippers. No cash, no ticket. Robertson thought back to the last time he'd taken the train without remembering to buy his ticket first and without enough cash to cover it, the way he'd pretended to be asleep and later moved throughout the cars in a successful bid to avoid the conductor. No chance of that here, he surmised.

Sheepishly, he spoke for the first time since he arrived here. "I'm sorry. I seem not to have it."

"I'm afraid I can't let you through without the fare." The old man seemed to genuinely feel bad about it. The two of them stood in silence for a few moments, Robertson pondering their impasse while the boatman stroked his wispy beard in a bemused manner.

The speechless standoff didn't last long before Robertson heard what sounded like hundreds of footsteps behind him. He turned to see twenty-some men in military regalia, clearly divided into two groups by their uniforms and the general tones of their skin. The first group brushed past Robertson with little reaction. The old man gave them the same smile, then spoke in some tongue Robertson didn't recognize. In turn, each man quietly handed over a silver coin, some wiping them from their eyes like dried tears, others plucking them from their tongues like wads of used-up gum.

With a frail finger, the boatman motioned the other group of soldiers forward. To them, he spoke English, but with a thick accent, warning that their fares would be slightly higher, what with exchange rates and all. The men paid him in kind and boarded the boat, which seemed to Robertson to expand its girth to accommodate the number of passengers. They boarded silently and solemnly, keeping some distance from their new shipmates.

As the oar hit the water and the boat shoved off, Robertson found himself again alone on the shore, and began searching the ground for coins. Only then did he realize the ground had no sand, nor any of the other materials he expected to see along a riverside. There was nothing to dig or sift through, no stretch moistened or eroded by the tide, just a clay-like terrain that didn't move. This ground was all a bleak grey, a backdrop against which any dropped change would have been immediately visible, but for all his effort he could see nothing shiny amid the muck. Increasingly frustrated, he got on his hands and knees, nearly crawling as he carefully scoured the ground for a fare, careful not to shred his pajamas in the process.

ANIMAL HUSBANDRY

When he arose, he turned to find an old man standing
there, huddled and shaking a bit in his overcoat. Robertson gave
him his friendliest smile, hoping that this stranger might hold
the solution to his troubles.

"Excuse me, sir," he inquired, realizing he instinctively said
it in a whisper, as if this could prove dangerous. "By any chance
could you spare..." The old man, who had stood inertly stoic,
simply shot him an angry glance and practically seethed the
word "nyet" before returning to his straight-ahead stare. Within
seconds the boat returned, the man paid and boarded, and the
boatman steered the craft away. This time he didn't even ask
Robertson for his payment; it was almost as if he'd become
invisible, or at least existed outside the man's peripheral vision.

Again Robertson stood alone on the shore, this time for a
very long while. He did all he could to occupy the time, continuing to search the ground in vain, scanning the full expanse of
the dank water before him. He considered exploring the land
behind him, but something warned him against wandering off.
He thought of his sister, who had once wandered off in a shopping mall and was lost for several hours, and how as a result his
parents never let him shop alone until he entered his late teens.
For the rest of his life, he'd been overly cautious about
wandering alone. Even when he got the paper in the morning,
he always told his landlady that he was leaving. They'd never
been close, exactly, but she kept an eye out for him. He
wondered what she was thinking about while he thought of
ways to entertain himself here.

Robertson couldn't be sure of how much time was passing,
not exactly. He never felt a need to sleep and his facial hair had
ceased to grow, so it was hard to track the days, but it felt like
several went by while he waited. People continued to appear
on his side of the water. Some alone, some in small groups,
some in a steady trickle of humanity and, one time, in a

hundreds-large clump. Men, women, and even children of all ages, all races, all arriving as suddenly as he had. None of these people ever tried to converse with him, and his attempts to approach them were usually met with looks of confusion, languages he couldn't comprehend, or the occasional sharp glance and curt word.

It never took long from the time the people arrived for the rickety boat to appear, the hunched old man rowing over slowly, but methodically. Everyone save Robertson had the requisite fare, boarded the boat in silence, and eventually went across the water. The oarsman occasionally gave Robertson that same toothy grin and asked if he'd come up with the money, but never seemed surprised by the negative reply. Days and weeks, or at least what Robertson perceived as days and weeks, continued in this same manner, different in the small details, but fundamentally the same.

After some undetermined amount of time, three people appeared on the shore next to Robertson. Two were older men, while the third was a woman roughly his own age. He realized right away that she was rather beautiful. Maybe he wouldn't have thought so before, but he had seen so few beautiful women since he wound up here, and she was the first to even acknowledge him, even if it was only a vague look of recognition in her eye. As always, the boat arrived soon, and the strangers paid their carriage.

Until the woman went to speak. Robertson discovered a strange sensation approaching joy when he heard her tell the boatman, "I'm sorry. I seem not to have it." He watched as the boatman gave her the same pitiful reply he'd received when he'd turned up penniless, and watched the boat turn and sail away.

After a few moments, the woman came over to him and, for the first time since he got there, someone began to engage

Robertson in a conversation that didn't focus on his lack of money.

"What's out there?" she asked him, pointing to the seemingly endless stretch of land behind him.

"I don't know," he admitted, not even bothering with an introduction. Looking at her, though, he realized that he suddenly wanted to know — that he wanted something to talk about with her. He realized his curiosity was beginning to overcome his inherent fear of the grey expanse.

She gave him a small grin as she started walking, slowly at first, into the fog.

He watched her nervously, as he saw his one source of even temporary companionship about to disappear over the horizon. The nervousness, the richest real emotion he'd felt in some time, dissipated as soon as she turned and reached out her hand. "Would you care to join me?" she asked, looking at her destination and back at him.

He approached, and gently took her hand in his, noticing that her palm, while mostly cold like his, still held a little bit of warmth in its center. He smiled, and felt some of the heaviness leave his tired eyes.

With that, they set off into the land beyond the shore, and Robertson became generally interested in where they would go, what they would explore, what kinds of dangers and opportunities they would face as they explored this unknown land.

He didn't care if it took a hundred years.

ABOUT THE AUTHOR

Jeff Fleischer's fiction has appeared in more than seventy publications including the *Chicago Tribune's Printers Row Journal, Shenandoah,* the *Saturday Evening Post,* and *So It Goes* by the Kurt Vonnegut Museum and Library.

He is also the author of non-fiction books including "Votes of Confidence: A Young Person's Guide to American Elections" (Zest Books, 2016, 2020, and 2024), "A Hot Mess: How the Climate Crisis is Changing Our World" (Zest Books, 2021), "Rockin' the Boat: 50 Iconic Revolutionaries" (Zest Books, 2015), and "The Latest Craze: A Short History of Mass Hysterias" (Fall River Press, 2011). His journalism has appeared in *Mother Jones,* the *Sydney Morning Herald,* the *Chicago Tribune, Chicago Magazine, Mental Floss, National Geographic Traveler,* and dozens of other local, national and international publications.

He lives in Chicago, Illinois.

ACKNOWLEDGMENTS

I want to take this opportunity to thank a bunch of people, without whom this book wouldn't have happened. Acknowledgement sections like this can't help but be incomplete, but I wanted to make sure to say "thank you":

To Lisa Kastner, Benjamin White, and the team at Running Wild Press for agreeing to publish this collection, believing in the book, and making it a reality. It has been an absolute pleasure working with them throughout this process.

To Elizabeth Taylor for accepting the story *Animal Husbandry* as one of the first chapbooks the *Chicago Tribune* published through *Printers Row* back in 2012. It was the first time I'd submitted a fiction story, and having it selected for such a great publication was a big reason why I kept writing fiction and why this book exists. To Meredith Cummings, Fiona Duffy, and the whole *So It Goes* team at the Kurt Vonnegut Museum and Library, Jessika St. Clair at the *Saturday Evening Post*, Lisa Duff at Pendust Radio, and Lise Quintana at Zoetic Press for all being repeat publishers of my stories, and to every single one of the literary magazines that have published my fiction. Each story acceptance still feels special, and I'm lucky to be associated with so many wonderful publications.

To the awesome team at Lerner Books and Zest Books, who have given my nonfiction books a good home for nearly a decade, and to all the readers, educators, and reviewers who have supported those books.

To my writing group of David Nelson, Gabriella Bonamici, Jamie Witherby, and Kira Bell, who were the first sets of eyes on several of these stories and many others. To Marsha Cook for encouraging me to explore creative writing and for all her help and advice through the years. To Jeff Meredith, Jeff Rose, Mark Greer, and Jean Henegan for decades of friendship and support in writing as well as in life. To Bob Gosman and Kathryn Knapp for being editors back in college and friends ever since. They're all fantastic writers whose work you should definitely check out, and whose feedback and support have been invaluable. And to all the other wonderful people I've been lucky enough to call my friends. There's a proverb that a man is best judged by the company he keeps, and I very much hope that's true.

To all the teachers who encouraged me along the way, especially Dee Gibson at Walden Elementary, Elaine Silberman at the Deerfield Park District, David Hirsch, Jeff White, and Susan Hebson at Deerfield High School, Irving Katz at Indiana University, and David Standish at Medill. Whatever ability they saw in me, I can't thank them enough for helping me develop it.

To my adorable puppy, Matilda, for keeping me company while I write and edit my work, and for making sure I have fun every day.

And, of course, to my incredible wife, Katie, for making my real life the best possible story, one better than anything I could have imagined.

Running Wild Press publishes stories that cross genres with great stories and writing. RIZE publishes great genre stories written by people of color and by authors who identify with other marginalized groups. Our team consists of:

Lisa Diane Kastner, Founder and Executive Editor
Cody Sisco, Acquisitions Editor, RIZE
Benjamin White, Acquisition Editor, Running Wild
Peter A. Wright, Acquisition Editor, Running Wild
Resa Alboher, Editor
Angela Andrews, Editor
Sandra Bush, Editor
Ashley Crantas, Editor
Rebecca Dimyan, Editor
Abigail Efird, Editor
Aimee Hardy, Editor
Henry L. Herz, Editor
Cecilia Kennedy, Editor
Barbara Lockwood, Editor
Scott Schultz, Editor
Evangeline Estropia, Product Manager
Kimberly Ligutan, Product Manager
Lara Macione, Marketing Director
Joelle Mitchell, Licensing and Strategy Lead
Pulp Art Studios, Cover Design
Standout Books, Interior Design
Polgarus Studios, Interior Design

Learn more about us and our stories at www.runningwildpress. com/rize

Loved this story and want more? Follow us at www.running wildpress.com/rize,

www.facebook.com/RW-Prize,
on Twitter @rizerwp and Instagram @rizepress